Cover Copy

One soul bound mate...one quest to find her.

Year 1210, Scottish Highlands.

Kidnapped as a wee lass by a fierce Highland chief, Kyla MacKenzie has been raised for the past twenty years as the chief's foster daughter, the ruthless chief a man who threatened to kill her parents should she ever speak the truth about her abduction. The chief covets her fae blood and when she's asked to tend to a captured enemy warrior and discovers they hold a soul bond, all her secrets could be exposed and her parents' lives endangered.

Warrior Ronan Matheson discovers his chosen one is the foster daughter of his clan's greatest enemy, a lass he's been searching for his entire life, although when his fellow warriors come to his rescue and he escapes from within the enemy's walls, he must then turn around and find a way to get back in, and all without his actual identity being discovered. It's time to bind his chosen one to him, and for her to learn all about her true clan.

Theirs is a battle of lost love, of passion flaring hot and strong, and of a journey to bridge the gap between two warring clans.

Books by Joanne Wadsworth

The Matheson Brothers Series
Highlander's Desire, Book One
Highlander's Passion, Book Two
Highlander's Seduction, Book Three
Highlander's Kiss, Book Four
Highlander's Heart, Book Five
Highlander's Sword, Book Six
Highlander's Bride, Book Seven
Highlander's Caress, Book Eight
Highlander's Touch, Book Nine
Highlander's Shifter, Book Ten
Highlander's Claim, Book Eleven
Highlander's Courage, Book Twelve
Highlander's Mermaid, Book Thirteen

Highlander Heat Series
Highlander's Castle, Book One
Highlander's Magic, Book Two
Highlander's Charm, Book Three
Highlander's Guardian, Book Four
Highlander's Faerie, Book Five
Highlander's Champion, Book Six
Highlander's Captive (Short Story)

Billionaire Bodyguards Series
Billionaire Bodyguard Attraction, Book One
Billionaire Bodyguard Boss, Book Two
Billionaire Bodyguard Fling, Book Three

Books by Joanne Wadsworth

Regency Brides Series
The Duke's Bride, Book One
The Earl's Bride, Book Two
The Wartime Bride, Book Three
The Earl's Secret Bride, Book Four
The Prince's Bride, Book Five
Her Pirate Prince, Book Six

Princesses of Myth Series
Protector, Book One
Warrior, Book Two
Hunter (Short Story - Included in Warrior, Book Two)
Enchanter, Book Three
Healer, Book Four
Chaser, Book Five
Pirate Princess, Book Six

Highlander's Bride

The Matheson Brothers, Book Seven

JOANNE WADSWORTH

Highlander's Bride
ISBN-13: 978-1-99-003437-4
Copyright © 2016, Joanne Wadsworth
Cover Art by Joanne Wadsworth
First electronic publication: March 2016

Joanne Wadsworth
http://www.joannewadsworth.com

AUTHOR'S NOTE:
This book is a work of fiction. The names, characters, places, and incidents are products of the writer's imagination or have been used fictitiously and are not to be construed as real. Any resemblance to persons, living or dead, actual events, locale or organizations is entirely coincidental. The author does not have any control over and does not assume any responsibility for third-party websites or their content.

Published in the United States of America

First digital publication: March 2016
First print publication: March 2016

The Fae Village

In the ninth century, the faerie king's youngest son visited a village along the shores of Loch Alsh and fell in love with the chief's daughter. The two wed and together created a half-blooded line born with the skills of the fae, a loyal line known as clan Matheson, a line guarded by the immortal fae princess, Cherub.

The Abduction

The fae village, on the shores of Loch Alsh, Scotland, 1190.

In the dark of night, Christina Matheson tried to push the foul-smelling gag from her mouth with her tongue, struggled and writhed against the bindings knotted around her wrists and ankles, but only managed to tighten them further. She wanted to scream, to claw at the warrior who'd snatched her from her home while her parents had slept so close by.

"Be still, child." A fearsome growl rumbled from the warrior as he carried her through the gate in the high stone wall surrounding her village. He searched both directions along the mist-shrouded loch then keeping to the shadows of the wall, slunk around to the rear. Into the copse of pines behind her home, he ducked and with a sly smile marched along the forest trail.

A jagged scar cut through the warrior's eyebrow, and she stilled as memories surged. She'd never mistake this man, not when she'd met him only a few days earlier. While Papa had been away with their Matheson warriors and all within their village had slept, Mama had borrowed a fisherman's skiff from a secluded corner of the bay and sailed them to this warrior's stronghold farther along the loch.

Mama hadn't had a choice in secreting them away that night, not when her fae skill of death-warning had reared to full and vibrant life. She'd received a vision, sensed death looming for another and immediately hastened to pass along the warning. As she'd rowed, Mama had whispered in her ear, "We leave because two young innocent lads are about to lose their lives and I know these boys well, love Coll and Duncan, just as I love you. I cannae allow their deaths to occur, even though they're our enemy's sons and reside within his keep."

"How did you come to love them?" She'd shuffled closer to Mama on the center bench seat, the cool of the night wrapping around her. Mama adored children and they flocked to her. Mayhap these two boys had too.

"The last time I saw Coll and Duncan they'd just turned three, so it's been five years since I was last with them. Even though the lads are MacKenzies, they hold fae blood, no' that their father allows any to know of it. I am one of the few, and now I've told you, you too must keep what you've learnt a secret, even from your papa." Mama raised the sail and sent them cruising faster along the waterway toward their enemy's lair.

Driven to understand more, she touched Mama's mind with hers. Her fae mind-walker skill always ensured her curiosity rang strong and even though she was young, being able to catch another's thoughts had certainly gifted her with a wisdom far beyond her short number of years. Carefully, she searched deeper within Mama's thoughts and gasped at the sadness overwhelming her beloved parent.

Mama squeezed her tight to her side, ran one hand over her mop of golden-red curls. "Never forget that those of fae blood can sense when you touch our minds, so during this trip you're no' to touch the mind of any MacKenzie. Over the centuries there has been the odd marriage between our clans since we have no' always been at war with each other, and those MacKenzies with even a trace of fae blood in their line might be able to sense your presence, just as I can right now. If any of our enemy discovered you hold a coveted fae skill, danger would lurk. Do you understand?"

"Aye, no touching my mind to that of a MacKenzie, or allowing them to know I hold a fae skill." She'd always been so thirsty for knowledge, and learning from others by reading their thoughts had aided her in quenching that thirst. But tonight she'd take all care, do exactly as Mama had said and not touch another's mind. "Since Coll and Duncan hold fae blood, who is their mama?"

"Their mother was a close childhood friend of mine. At the age of eight and ten Beth Matheson left for Colin MacKenzie's keep to visit a relative and no' long afterward handfasted with one of the MacKenzie's warriors, or so we were told. I soon learnt the truth. Several months after Beth wed, I received a missive from her and in it she pleaded for me to come to her. I sailed down this very waterway and once I arrived was taken upstairs to Beth's chamber. That's when Beth poured out her heart to me. I discovered that day exactly whom she'd handfasted with and it wasnae one of the chief's warriors, but the chief himself. Colin MacKenzie."

"Why the secret?"

"Colin is well known for his deviousness, but she believed herself in love with him, and Colin in love with her. Their match was one her parents would never have allowed, so she lied, although unfortunately she soon discovered his true nature too, and when she told him she intended to return to her kin, he instead locked her away in her chamber and allowed only one single maid entry. The MacKenzie never intended to wed her proper once their handfast of a year and a day was done, no' when he was already betrothed to the chief's daughter of the neighboring MacLennan clan. His agreement with the MacLennan was one that couldnae be broken, and once he'd gotten Beth with child, he had exactly what he'd always secretly desired, to have the revered Matheson fae blood running through his direct line, as well as a bride-to-be of MacLennan blood with whom he'd soon wed."

"Why was she permitted to send for you, Mama?"

"I was granted permission to visit because Beth and I both held the same skill of death-warning, and unfortunately she'd seen her own death in a vision and hoped I might be able to halt it. Although there wasnae a chance I could, her bleeding naught that I could stem after she went into labor and delivered her sons." Mama hugged her tighter to her side. "Afore Beth breathed her last, she asked if I should ever see death hovering over either Coll or Duncan, then to do all I could to ensure their survival. I gave her my word I would and gladly did so." Mama sniffed, the sadness in her eyes making her heart tug. "I grieved for Beth terribly after she passed away. Her sons had lost a mother they'd never know, but worse, after Beth's passing I also saw her sons' death in a vision should I no' remain with them. They were so sickly as first, born almost two months too soon." Mama lifted her gaze to the twinkling stars in the night sky. "Following the boys' birth, I remained as their nurse and cared for them, just as Beth would have wished for me to do."

An owl hooted within the dark depths of the forest rising high either side of the channel and she rubbed her cheek against Mama's warm arm. She would hate to lose her mama as these boys had lost theirs. "What happened next?"

"Within days of Beth's death, Colin sent for the MacLennan lass and the two spoke vows, her dowry and lands quickly added to his so he might strengthen his own holdings. He didnae mourn Beth and I hated him for it, decided I would ensure her sons knew of their mother, only he halted my ability to do even that. Should I have spoken out, he threatened to send his warriors to our village and slay as many as he could. He had no desire to lose the lands he'd gained by incurring the MacLennan's wrath, and his intentions rang true, a vision assailing me right then and there should I speak the truth to my own kinsmen. So many innocent lives would have been lost. I couldnae utter a word, have never been able to do so in all these years, no' with either Beth's parents or your papa. None are aware of the truth, other than me, and such guilt consumes me because of the secrets, but that is how things must be."

"You've now told me." The moon slid behind a darkened cloud then reemerged.

"Aye, because I saw you in my vision along with the boys this eve. You're supposed to come with me, although I have no understanding of why." Mama shrugged. "Sometimes that is the way of my skill."

"I give you my word, Mama, that I'll never tell another of their fae blood. Your secret is safe with me."

"Aye, as I knew it would be." Love shone in Mama's eyes. "I often wish I could have returned to the boys afore now, but that's been impossible due to the continued feuding."

"Tell me more about them." 'Twas so sad the boys had no knowledge of their fae blood, had never had the chance to visit their mother's kin at the village.

"Colin's wife, Cait, sat with the boys and I often. She adored them, and afore too long the MacKenzie claimed Cait was their mother and none refuted the fact, no' even her. His word was accepted as the truth and Beth became all but forgotten by those few who'd known her at his keep." Waves sloshed against the hull and Mama softly sighed. "Soon, Cait too conceived and once she had, Colin sent her away to Rhue Castle to give birth, one of his northernmost strongholds. Tensions were tight between the clans at the time and he wanted her as far away from the hostilities as possible. There within the safety of Rhue's walls, she delivered his son and named him Jeremiah, although she remained at Rhue for quite some time afterward, what with the escalation of the feuding at the time."

The wind rose, slapped into the sail and sent them skimming the waves faster. "When did you leave and return to the village?"

"I was forced to leave the year the boys turned three or else become a pawn in the war between our clans."

"Is that when you met Papa?"

"Aye." Mama smiled and through Christina's connection to Mama's mind, she caught the image of Papa standing within the inner courtyard of Matheson House. Papa's pale hair lay damp against his head from his training session, and Mama appeared so very tiny standing next to him. The images continued to flow. Papa curled one arm around Mama's back, dipped his head and kissed her, right there next to the center well draped in ivy. Mama's thoughts swarmed with love.

"My bond with your papa took very quickly and we soon spoke vows. You arrived within the year, finally giving me a child of my own to care for, and no' a child I would ever have to leave behind as I left Coll and Duncan."

She nestled deeper into Mama's side, the wind nipping at her nose and fingertips, turning them numb with the cold. "Yours is a very important skill, Mama, one that saves lives."

"My skill is both a burden and a privilege. Here, let me warm you up." From her traveling sack, Mama pulled a plaid out and bundled her in the added layer of soft wool before rubbing her arms and kissing her cheeks. "Is that better?"

"Aye, and thank you for explaining everything to me." She pulled her mind back and left Mama's thoughts behind.

Up ahead, the MacKenzie's castle rose like a fortress within the dark. A touch of moonlight shimmered over the stronghold built on an island a stone's throw from the mainland. The massive gray tower windows were lit with candles, and torches along the ramparts cast their glow high over the fortified walls. Guardsmen patrolled the barbican in heavy battle attire. So well-guarded.

Mama gazed toward the imposing sight, lowered the sail and picked up the oars then rowed them toward the sea-gate. Leaning closer, Mama whispered, "Do you see that guard standing on duty near the stairs, the one with the bushy red beard?"

"Aye." Such a big bear of a man he was.

"That is Gregor, the MacKenzie's most trusted captain, the only man at the keep who knows the truth about Coll and Duncan's birth. He is extremely loyal to his chief, yet was also rather kind to me during my stay. A touch of fae blood runs somewhere within his line, but 'tis several generations removed and he sensed a kinship with me. I shall ask him to take us to the MacKenzie, although while we're here, you're to remain right by my side. No wandering about, and remember my earlier warning."

"Aye, no touching the mind of another while we're here." She wriggled within the layers of wool.

"I love you, my sweet, always and forever."

"I love you too, Mama, always and forever." With more love than her little heart could hold at times.

"Gregor!" Mama called out and lifted a hand. "I come in peace."

"Is that you, Grace?" Hand raised to his forehead, the warrior wearing thick fur boots and a two-handed claymore strapped to his back, squinted through the dark. "What on earth are you doing here, and out on the water so late at night?"

"I've had a vision and must speak to Colin. Your chief and his sons must hear what I have to say this night." Mama scooped her onto her lap.

"One moment. I'll take you to the chief myself." Gregor whistled to two of his fellow warriors who waded into the water, gripped the sides of their skiff and guided their boat the last few feet until it nestled next to the stone stairs.

Settled in Mama's arms, she snuggled as Mama stepped onto the landing.

Up the sea-gate stairs, Mama walked and at the top, Gregor gestured for them to proceed him through the postern gate. They did and Mama crossed the gravelly inner courtyard and halted under the high arch of the front door, set Christina down on her feet and as she stepped inside, glanced over her shoulder. "Stay close."

With a quick nod, she followed Mama into the great hall.

The blazing fireplace spread its warmth and sent its flicking orange and red glow all about. Trestle tables had been pushed to one side to allow more room for the warriors who'd bedded down on pallets to rest for the night. The drone of their snores echoed all about, while on the far side of the hall, narrow windows rose almost to the ceiling and tapestries covered the stone walls in between the panes of pretty colored stained glass. She tramped across a wealth of rushes scattered across the floor and smiled at a brown dog with floppy ears as he rubbed against a table leg to ease an itchy side.

A barefoot lad in brown breeches and a dirt-smeared tunic, his eyes barely visible under his mop of black hair, crouched in the corner near one of the sleeping warriors. With a wedge of bread in his hands, he stuffed it into his mouth and chewed. She stepped closer, just as a lass dashed out from a shadowed side stairwell and in her blue kirtle and slippers, knelt next to the lad and handed him a sweet pastry.

The boy gobbled it down and the girl, her red locks tumbling in curls to her waist, offered her a welcoming smile and bounced across to her. "Are you hungry too? I can find you some food."

"Nay, I've eaten well this day. I'm Christina."

"I'm Fiona, the daughter of Gregor." She motioned to the warrior disappearing with Mama down the darkened passageway at the rear of the great hall. "My father."

"Oh, I must catch Mama up. She told me to remain close."

"Then come." Fiona hooked her arm through hers and skipped toward the passageway.

At the chief's solar door, Gregor knocked and called out, "I bring a visitor, Chief."

"Come in."

"Follow me." Gregor opened the door.

Mama lifted her chin and stepped inside the chief's inner sanctum.

"I must go." She smiled at Fiona and hauling the trailing ends of her plaid closer, shuffled in behind Mama. The solar held padded armchairs in a beautiful blue and gold thread and a large round table sat to one side. A lady wearing layers of rich golden velvet, the bodice cut dangerously low, rose from one of the padded chairs, bent over the chief at his massive oak desk and murmured something in his ear.

"Aye, wench, I'll be with you soon." The MacKenzie slapped the lady's rear, and she giggled and sashayed out the door.

"Shh, this I cannae miss," Fiona whispered as she snuck past her then ducked under the table and scuttled into the shadows.

Clutching Mama's green woolen skirts, she peeked around her. A single lit candle on the MacKenzie's desk cast its light over the chief's weathered face and made the scar zigzagging through one of his thick eyebrows glow a grizzly red. Dressed in a belted plaid and loose-sleeved black tunic, he rose from his desk, his gaze flickering with intrigue as he crossed to Mama.

"Well, well," he crooned as he halted in front of them. "This is an unexpected visit, Grace. It's been five years. Whatever brings you here so late in the night, and unattended at that?"

"You know of my skill. Of those who live but are soon to die, I receive a vision." Mama lifted one eyebrow, her voice firm and showing no sign of any unease. "You're also aware of my promise to Beth, and tonight I'm here to honor that promise to my dearest friend."

"Aye, Beth." Teeth gritted, a low growl rumbled from him. "No one is permitted to speak her name within these walls, but I'll allow you to do so this one time. Tell me of your vision."

"'Tis the lads who need to hear of what I've seen. 'Tis imperative."

"I see." The chief scraped a hand along his bristly jaw, slowly nodded and eyed Gregor standing at attention to the side of the solar. "Wake my sons and bring them here. I'll nay have any harm befall them."

"Aye, Chief." Gregor left and the chief tapped one foot, his gaze moving from Mama to her. "Who is the child?"

"My daughter, Christina."

"Is she skilled?"

"Nay, and no' all of the fae are skilled, as you well know." Mama tucked her more fully in behind her.

Footsteps clomped down the corridor and Gregor returned with two sleepy-eyed lads trailing behind him. He nudged the lads forward to stand before their chief and Mama. Dressed in braies and loose tunics that reached their knees, they both tugged up woolen socks a few sizes too big for their feet. The boys appeared similar, although not identical. She could tell them apart, although who was who, she couldn't wait to learn.

"Speak as you need to, Grace, but you'll do so with me noting your every word." The chief pushed an ink bottle and quill to the center of his desk and perched on the front edge as he eyed his sons. "Coll, Duncan, this is Mistress Grace from the fae village. She brings you a message you must heed."

"More than a message." With a tender smile, Mama lowered to her knees before the two boys. "'Tis so good to see you both. You must be Coll?" She grasped the hands of the lad on the left, the boy's dark hair framing his face and prominent chin. "Your brown eyes are flecked with gold, just as they were at your birth."

"Grace." The chief thumped one fisted hand on his desk and rattled the dagger resting near the edge. "Tell them what you've seen and no more."

"They must learn the full truth in order to heed my word, unless you wish for the death of your sons."

"You intend to speak more in-depth about Beth?"

"I must in this case."

"Damn it." He fisted his hands then muttered, "Fine. Say what you will. None within this solar will utter a word after you've left."

"Thank you." Mama looked at both boys. "I hold the fae skill of death-warning and can receive visions. Of those who live but are soon to die, I can warn them aforehand and ensure they are given the chance to live. Earlier this eve, I had a vision of both of you."

"I remember you." Coll peered into Mama's eyes, such wisdom shining within his young gaze. "You cared for us when we were little."

"Aye, you and Duncan were all but three years of age when I left."

"I remember you too." The lad on the right, his hair as dark as Coll's, but his eyes a clear blue, inched forward a step. "I'm Duncan. What have you seen, Mistress Grace?"

"More than I wish." Mama cleared her throat. "In order to ensure your survival you must both listen to me well. From this day forth, neither of you must ever raise a hand in battle against a Matheson, no' because you willnae be strong warriors, but because in harming a Matheson you will also be harming yourselves. Soon, you will both understand what I speak of, for there will be things you'll be able to do that no other MacKenzie warrior can. The fae battle skill will come upon you and when it does your strength will be immense."

"We're MacKenzies, no' Mathesons. How can we hold a fae skill?" Coll glanced at his father. "Mother was a MacLennan and no' of fae blood."

"What's going on, Father?" Duncan darted a look back and forth between Mama and the chief.

"I never wished to speak of this, no' since you both took your mother's death so hard."

"Cait has passed?" Shock coursed across Mama's face as she rose to her feet.

"Aye, she took a chest illness last winter. She's been gone nigh on a year now." Colin MacKenzie shoved off the desk and paced the solar then halted before his sons. "Since I no longer have any choice but to speak of this, I shall. Unfortunately, Cait wasnae your true mother. Afore your birth, I handfasted with a fae lass named Beth, although she passed away while birthing you both. Mistress Grace was here at the time of your true mother's passing and she took care of you until 'twas time for her to return to her own people at the village. The knowledge of your fae blood isnae something I speak of, ever, and neither of you are permitted to speak of it either, or your coming skill." The war braids plaited at each side of his head swayed as he lowered to his haunches. "You are my sons, hold my blood, and your additional strength will be attributed to that fact alone. Do you both understand? I certainly cannae lose the alliance I've formed with the MacLennan, or the land I've come by."

"Aye, Father," both murmured together.

"There is more," Mama continued, the plea in her eyes clear to see as she eyed Colin. "You must ensure Coll and Duncan are taught the arts of warfare well. One day, far in the future, they will meet a fae sorceress by the name of Muirin. I saw her in my vision. She is the one who'll ensure your sons fulfil their destiny."

"What destiny?"

"All I can say is, 'tis time for the fae to live."

"Nay, 'tis time for clan MacKenzie to live." Jaw clenched, the MacKenzie shoved toward Mama and Christina rushed forward and kicked the chief's shin. No one would hurt her mama and get away with it.

The chief bellowed and tried to grab her, only Mama scooped her up and snapped at him, "You promised I'd always be safe should I need to return with a vision, but now 'tis clearly time I left. Look after Beth's sons, and never forget my vision." Mama fled out the door and Christina clutched her around the neck, her chin bumping on Mama's shoulder.

At his doorway, the chief snarled, the look of retribution in his gaze flaring strong.

Never had she been so scared of a man, or at least not until this night. Colin MacKenzie had struck terror into her very heart once again.

"Cease your whimpering, child." Colin stormed down the darkened forest trail as he left her fae village well behind. He should never have snuck into her home and taken her from her parents. Never. He rounded a corner then dumped her into the waiting arms of one of his warriors. Gregor, Fiona's father.

The MacKenzie's second-in-command shook his head at her. "Stay still. Dinnae make a sound. All will go far easier if you do."

She tried once again to spit the foul tasting gag from her mouth but it remained bound firmly in place. There would be no escaping her capture, not this night.

Looming over her, the MacKenzie plucked his dagger from his wrist sheath, gripped her hair and sliced it off at the root. He stuffed the mass of golden-red curls into his sporran then covered her head in a heavy black veil. "Now no one shall ever learn who you are, and if you wish for your parents to live then you'll forget your village and all who remain within it. From this moment forth, you'll no longer be Christina Matheson but instead Kyla MacKenzie, my foster daughter. You have no fae blood, no kin, and I've taken you in, a poor urchin I found abandoned in the forest. You'll join me, be raised within my household and even though you remain unskilled, in time I'll ensure your revered fae blood mixes into my direct line. You'll wed one of my three sons, whichever I please. Do you understand?"

"Aye," she mumbled through the cloth.

She tried to cross the distance to Mama and Papa and connect with them, only she couldn't. They were too far away. Tears streamed down her cheeks. Never would she endanger her parents' lives. More tears fell, endlessly.

Cherub – The Fae Princess and Guardian of her Earthbound Kind

Clan Matheson fae village, Loch Alsh, Scotland, 1210, twenty years later.

Under the midnight brilliance of the night sky twinkling with a myriad of stars, Cherub walked arm and arm with Kirk along the pebbly shoreline nestled before the village. The wind rushed all around, fluttering her white fur cloak about her legs and sending her blond hair streaming past her shoulders. Something within the wind tickled her fae senses and she halted, raised her arms and allowed the *air*—the element she controlled—to bring to her the secrets it held.

As an immortal time-walker and her fae people's princess, 'twas her duty to aid those of her fae-blooded kind who walked this Earth and she did so by ensuring the newly soul bound were brought together, no matter what divide of time separated them. With her time-walker ability, she could open portals if she wished, could travel great distances through time, to wherever she was most needed.

"Do you sense lost souls this night?" Kirk, her soul bound

mate, stepped in behind her, slid his arms around her waist and nuzzled her neck. With his big body curved around hers, he warmed her through with his heavenly heat.

"I do, and between two of our fae kind who live right here in this time, although one is currently visiting your clan at Ivanson Castle in the twenty-first century."

"You're speaking of Ronan?"

"I am." A month past, she and Kirk had rescued Ronan from deep within the dungeons of Carron Castle, the stronghold belonging to Coll MacKenzie. She'd opened a portal and taken Ronan directly to a doctor at Ivanson in order for him to heal as he'd needed to from his extensive injuries. "The other I sense is Kyla."

"The lass Ronan met while imprisoned in Carron's cells, the lass he believes was kidnapped by Colin as a child from the fae village?"

"Aye, Christina was taken from us twenty years ago and even though we searched high and low for her following her disappearance, we never found her, never knew who'd taken her, never received a note requesting a demand of coin either. Ronan is desperate to return to Kyla and we need to ensure he reaches her without issue, particularly while she is with her foster brother and far away from Colin MacKenzie's evil clutches."

"I see." Kirk nibbled on her ear. "A task I am more than ready for."

"As am I." She slid her hands underneath the hem of his white tunic and spread one palm over his heart. "Ronan's new identity is almost complete. Tavish adds the finishing touches as we speak and once he's done, we must ensure Ronan and Kyla have the chance for their bond to take form.

"A plan I'm in total agreement with." He dipped her backward, rubbed his cheek against hers, his love for her enveloping her in its fierce intensity. "I love you, would never be able to live without you, would hate it if you'd ever been stolen from me as Kyla was with Ronan. When do we leave?"

"First thing in the morn, and I love you too." She cupped his face in her hands, seized his mouth with hers and allowed the deep emotions she held for him to consume her. What remained of this night would be theirs, but once the sun rose on the morrow, they would be needed at Ivanson in the twenty-first century. Ronan would be awaiting them, ready and anxious to begin his hunt.

Aye, Ronan's coming journey would be one of immense trials and tribulations, a chase to bind his chosen one to him that would see the truth of Kyla's birth finally come to light. 'Twas time for Kyla to embrace her Matheson kin, to no longer be a lost child but returned to her loved ones, as she should have been so very long ago.

'Twas time to right the wrongs of the past, this journey one she couldn't wait to set in motion. Soon, very soon.

Chapter 1

Carron Castle, held by Coll MacKenzie, Scotland, 1210, the following day.

Kyla MacKenzie stood on the high rocky cliff overlooking the blue-green waters of the inner channel of Loch Carron as the dawn sun breached the horizon. A brisk breeze rose and whipped the brewing storm clouds farther out toward sea. If only the wind could whip her own unsettled emotions away just as quickly. For twenty years her true name of Christina Matheson had never been spoken again, and no man did she despise more than Colin MacKenzie who'd taken that right away from her. 'Twas just as well Coll and Duncan had brought her here for a little while, to give her a small reprieve from their chief and his devious demands.

"Come inside, Kyla!" Duncan leaned over the corner crenellation of the battlements, his great plaid belted at his waist and untucked tunic flapping in the breeze. "I must leave soon and wish to say farewell."

"Coming." The rising sun sent a swathe of vibrant gold and red shimmering across the curtain wall and she grasped her midnight-blue velvet skirts and hurried back through the main gate. Up on the battlements, Duncan tugged his leather riding gloves on and shrugged into his leather jerkin. She rushed up the side stairs. Since he was leaving, then their current chess game would need to be put on hold. Most nights they adjourned to the library and played together, the game one Coll had never had the patience for, but one she and Duncan most definitely had. She thrived on considering all the multiple strategies needed to win, always adored it when she managed to best Duncan in what many called the King's Game.

Breathing hard, she reached the top of the barbican then giggled as Duncan caught her up in his outstretched arms and twirled her around. "Put me down, you big oaf."

"Dinnae you go and move those chess pieces around while I'm gone, little sister. I know exactly what my next move shall be, although 'twill have to wait until my return afore I can make it." He set her back on her feet, his expression turning somber as he murmured in her ear, "You looked sad out there on the cliffs. My father is far away at his own keep and you're supposed to be enjoying yourself while staying here with Coll and I."

"Your father's threats follow me about no matter where I am. I also miss Coll. Have you heard any word from him?"

"Nay, but he'll be somewhere to the far north of our MacKenzie lands. Hopefully he'll send a messenger soon so we'll know exactly how his mission fares. Our fighting force isnae yet as strong as we'd like it. That's for certain." Duncan stroked one finger under her chin, lifted her gaze fully to his. "I love you, just as Coll loves you, and as your mother told us in her vision twenty years ago, 'tis time for the fae to live. That includes the three of us, even though you've never been able to return to your true clan."

"They're your true clan too, no matter you've never lived amongst them." She tapped his nose. "Where are you going?"

"I must ride for Ardan House to see how Niall Matheson's training goes under Muirin's guidance. There is much the fae sorceress can teach him, just as she's taught Coll and I."

"Are they getting along better, Muirin and Niall?"

"At first they argued night and day, but their soul bond is strong, has grown greatly this past month. 'Tis of course a shame Niall's son escaped our dungeons afore I could officially release him as I'd wished to do."

"Your guards beat Ronan to within an inch of his life and never should have. I'm glad his fae princess arrived and ensured his escape. I couldnae stand seeing him being so restrained behind our bars."

"I left implicit instructions that Ronan never came to any harm while I was gone and the two guards who flayed him have been sent away. I had no choice but to ensure his captivity. Hamish had 'seen' 'twas necessary if Muirin was to have a chance in strengthening her bond with Niall. I certainly willnae have any of my men bringing harm to one of the fae."

"The fae village has strong healers within." She'd prayed the fae princess had gotten Ronan safely into her people's hands.

"Aye, and they would've ensured Ronan's injuries healed without issue." His gaze softened as he tucked a lock of her golden-red hair behind her ear. "You've yet to tell me exactly what's worrying you. I wish only to chase your sadness away."

"I—" How she wanted to tell Duncan of the soul bond that had taken form between her and Ronan during his captivity, only doing so would be fruitless. Colin's threats remained in force, whether she was soul bound to another or not, and if she didn't abide by his will then her parents would pay dearly for it, something she'd never allow. With her silence, she'd been protecting them for the past twenty years and would continue to do so, for however long it took. Her future was set. She'd wed either Coll, Duncan, or Jeremiah. The MacKenzie's decree that she would rang strong in her ears, as it had since the day he'd issued it.

No one shall ever learn who you are, and if you wish for

your parents to live then you'll forget your village and all who remain within it. From this moment forth, you'll no longer be Christina Matheson but instead Kyla MacKenzie, my foster daughter. You have no fae blood, no kin, and I've taken you in, a poor urchin I found abandoned in the forest. You'll join me, be raised within my household and even though you remain unskilled, in time I'll ensure your revered fae blood mixes into my direct line. You'll wed one of my three sons, whichever I please. Do you understand?

Aye, she'd understood his decree well, would rather he choose between Coll or Duncan. She certainly shuddered at the thought of ever having to join with Jeremiah, Colin's one and only son by Cait. During his younger years, Jeremiah had lived both at Rhue Castle to the far north of his father's lands and also with them at Loch Alsh. He was cut from the same cloth as his father and she'd done her best to steer clear of him, however possible. At the age of ten, Colin had thankfully sent Jeremiah away to be fostered with the Chief of MacLennan and now Rhue belonged to him, a stronghold Jeremiah ruled with an iron hand.

Heart heaving, she clutched her aching chest. She had to take every advantage of this time she'd been given here, because if she wished even a little say in her future then she needed to take action.

"I can see your sadness grows." Duncan rubbed her arms, stroking slowly up and down with his gloved hands. "A burden shared is a burden lessened."

"Jeremiah has no knowledge of my fae blood, would take every advantage of it if he did." Colin had kept that a secret, never wishing for one of her kin to hear of the news and suspect who'd taken her.

"I agree, although neither Coll or I would ever share the truth about your fae blood with Jeremiah. In time, Father though might if he believes he'll gain from doing so." A slow nod. "I believe I understand where your sadness is coming from."

"May I tell you something?"

"Of course, anything."

She dragged in a deep, fortifying breath, the wind whipping around them. 'Twas time for all honesty. "If I had the chance to choose the man I'm to wed, then it would be you."

"Are you certain?"

"Very." Her throat dried out. "I wish to marry you."

"Then consider yourself betrothed." No hesitation.

"Pardon?"

"I've no wish to see you wed to Jeremiah, will do anything to ensure that never happens." He gripped her shoulders. "We've been foster brother and sister these past twenty years and of course I hold a brotherly love for you, but if we're both willing then we can change that."

"You truly think so?"

"Anything is possible." He smiled, one brow rising. "Come. We'll see if we can make the change. Permit me a kiss, to seal our agreement to wed."

"Is this a test?" She gulped.

"Aye, and you've gone a little green, Kyla." He stepped her backward into a nook where none could see them, his smile turning cheeky. "I promise no' to slobber all over you, provided you promise the same."

She laughed. "I promise."

"Now that's better. It hurts my heart to see you forced into a corner and to accept what must be, but I give you my word I'll be a good husband, to ensure you want for naught. And you're right to speak to me about all of this. We need to take the choice out of my father's hand and into ours then once we've wed and consummated our marriage, he'll be able to do naught about it."

"All I want to do is keep my parents safe, to make certain Colin never lays a hand on them."

"Then marrying me will ensure it, and upon my return from Ardan House, we'll speak our vows afore a priest. We'll be man and wife and when I lie with you, you'll give me your complete submission." His cheeky smile doubled. "Which means you'll allow me to win every game of chess to come."

"Never." She slapped his chest and he broke out into loud laughter. "Hurry up with that kiss. Slobber away and I shall do the same."

"Och, that's my lass, my devoted betrothed." He leaned closer and brushed his nose against hers, his breath warm and soft against her cheeks. "Close your eyes."

It might be best if she did.

Oh goodness. Kissing Duncan seemed the strangest thing to do. He'd taught her how to swim, even crafted her first bow from a long length of yew he'd whittled away at as a lad, then afterward he'd shown her how to shoot an arrow toward a target. Whenever she'd moaned about needing something sweet to eat, he'd been the one to sneak a treat from the kitchens, well him and Fiona both. When learning to ride, Duncan had been the one to spend hour upon hour teaching her how to sit in the saddle, to care for her horse and all other things. His devotion was absolute.

She took one long breath in then slowly let it out. She could do this. She closed her eyes and when she did, a sweet image of Ronan wavered to full brilliance in her mind. Ronan's pale blond hair brushed his shoulders, his scruffy beard the same pale shade and those bewitching eyes of his heating to such a stunning shade of liquid gold. Ronan had such a heavily muscled body, much like Duncan did, that of a warrior born and bred. Aye, Duncan was Ronan. That she needed to believe, to consider naught else if she wished to get through this kiss.

"Ready, Kyla?"

"Aye." A soft sweep of his lips over hers, his mouth there one moment then gone the next. She peeked one eye open. "Was that it?"

"For now." A devilish glint lit his eyes. "That wasnae so

bad, was it?"

"'Twas terrible for a first kiss, but glad I am 'tis over."

"Aye, glad I am too." He pulled her in for a long hug and she hugged him back, the familiarity of his hold soothing her. "Be good while I'm gone."

"I'll try, and travel safely. I shall see you upon your return."

"That you will, by the week's end and no more." He tweaked her nose, jogged down the side stairs toward the lad who held his destrier's reins in the inner bailey and mounted. With a wave, he rode out under the arch, a half dozen of his armed men falling in behind him. Ardan House, his own stronghold farther along the loch, sat close which meant Duncan was never far away.

She rubbed her chilled arms. Well, 'twas done. Betrothed now, and a traitor too, to her own mate no less. With a long sigh, she opened her skill and reached out along the pathway which would take her to Ronan, although as usual naught but a dark void remained in place where he should have been. Surely he'd survived the whipping inflicted by those awful guards. She certainly wouldn't consider anything else. He lived, would continue to live, provided he stayed far away from her.

Downstairs, she tramped and across the courtyard toward the front door of the keep.

The hearty chattering of her kin reverberated toward her as she stepped into the great hall where a good hundred warriors remained seated around the trestle tables as they ate their morning meal. Serving lasses weaved around the men with trays of steaming bowls of oats and jugs of warm cider in hand. Overhead, massive wooden-beamed rafters rose to an imposing height with the dawn's sunshine peppering in through the tall windows and sprinkling golden rays across the wooden floorboards. She walked past the blazing fireplace where two dogs sat guzzling scraps then stepped up onto the dais.

"It appears you've been out on the cliffs again. Your gown

is damp and your nose all red." Gordon rose from where he was seated and pulled out a chair for her. Duncan's captain had spent a great deal of time guarding Ronan in the dungeons, had come to know their prisoner well.

"I wished to see the sun rise and the storm clouds finally scatter." She sat in the high-backed chair and he tucked it in. "I spoke to Duncan afore he rode out and we, ah—" How did she put this? Best she just speak the words and be done with it. "We've agreed to a betrothal."

"Then you have my most hearty congratulations. Duncan will be good for you, lass." He returned to his seat, plunked down in his chainmail and black boots. From the platters in the center of the table, he selected some of the choicest cuts of meat and added them to his trencher then offered her the platter holding fresh fish.

"Thank you." She popped the meat into her mouth and it near melted on her tongue. 'Twas delicious, yet the taste soon turned to dust as another image of Ronan flittered through her mind. Arms outstretched, he'd been chained to the blackened stone wall of his cell, his body slumped and his hunger and thirst beating at her. It had taken all her willpower not to unlock those cuffs and set him free. How she'd wanted to, desperately. All that had stayed her hand was the knowledge that Muirin needed time with his father. The fae sorceress had deserved the chance to forge the soul bond with her mate and she'd had no desire to take that right from her, not as it had been so cruelly taken from her. 'Twas sacred, a bond all her kin desired. A bond she'd been gifted with, but could never accept.

Such sadness swirled within her heart, made it beat sluggish and slow. Her fingers and toes went all icy and numb. She squeezed her eyes shut and forced the dreaded emotions away. Plodding around the keep all maudlin and sorrowful would never do, not when word would soon spread of her betrothal with Duncan. Her kin needed to see her contentment, and Duncan deserved naught less than her full acceptance of their coming marriage.

"Would you care for some tea, my lady?" One of the maids set a bowl of oats before her.

"Aye, that would be wonderful, with a good spoonful of honey, please." Smiling at the maid, she curled her hands around the underside of the bowl of oats to warm her fingers.

"I'll be but a moment." The maid swished away, her dark hair bundled up under her frilly cap and her apron ties swaying down to her knees.

"What are your plans for the day now you're about to be a wedded woman?" Gordon shoved a bacon rasher into his mouth.

"I'd like to take a swim." That would certainly help clear the gloominess from her thoughts and rejuvenate her spirit. They'd left summer behind and autumn had well and truly taken ahold, winter a mere breath away, but she would take this opportunity to set her thoughts in order and a swim always did that.

"You'll need a guard. I'll take you to the loch myself."

"I dinnae mind going on my own. It isnae too far." She often walked the short distance to the pool without any issue, although with the blood feuds currently raging across the land and more enemy warriors about, such unease consumed them all. From the jug in the center of the dais, she added a dash of milk to her oats and ate a spoonful.

"I'll come with you. I cannae have Duncan tossing me into the dungeons for no' ensuring your complete care."

"Here ye are, my lady." The maid returned and set a cup of tea before her and she thanked her before she bustled away to serve the men at the closest table below their platform.

"How soon do you wish to go?" More bacon stuffed in his mouth, along with a slurp of his drink.

"As soon as possible, if you dinnae mind." She finished her meal, bid Gordon to await her by the postern gate and hurried upstairs to collect a few things from her chamber.

Plaid draped over one arm and a bar of soap and a drying cloth stuffed into her satchel, she hiked back downstairs and across the inner courtyard to where Gordon stood at the gate, his chainmail sparkling in the sunlight.

He motioned for her to go first and she skipped past him as the sun rose higher and warmed the earth. Across the open meadow, she tramped then ducked into the forest. She weaved in and around thick bushes before finally emerging at her favorite pool. The loch, small, secluded and surrounded with towering trees, offered a haven of respite and provided her with all she loved most about the Highlands, nature and all its abundance.

"I'll wait back along the trail to give you your privacy. Holler out if you need any aid and I'll come." Gordon vanished within the thickness of the trees, a snare in his hand. He'd hunt while she bathed.

Assured she remained alone, she loosened the front laces of her midnight-blue gown and wriggled the velvet over her hips. It shimmered to the ground and she stepped out of the pool of fabric, kicked her slippers off and curled her toes into the lush grass. With her shift's skirts brushing her legs, she picked up the bar of soap and stepped around the loch bordered by the odd protruding boulder and bounded up onto the ledge rimming the far edge.

Oh, how she'd adore a swim without any encumbrance, even that of her shift. She rocked from foot to foot. Sunlight streamed through the trees and dappled over the grass dotted with yellow flowers and the odd scrub of heather. Gordon had left and it wasn't as if anyone else was nearby. She also adored the sensation of the water flowing over her bare skin and once under the darkened surface, none could see below. Grinning, she set the soap down on the stony ledge, whipped her shift over her head, dropped it and dove into the dark depths of the pool.

Chilly water washed over her and she gasped at the icy

shock. Oh, how invigorating. She burst to the surface and laughed as the freedom of being so at one with nature rushed through her. This was exactly what she needed to raise her spirits and as the sun rose higher, she dipped and dived within the glorious water before floating on her back. Aye, she'd make the best of what she'd been given, and marrying Duncan would ensure her true heart's desire, that her parents lived. All that mattered was their survival. Always and forever.

* * * *

Never would Ronan Matheson allow Kyla to remain beyond his touch, not for another day. Over eight-hundred years in the future, he sat inside Tavish Matheson's medical rooms on the second floor of Ivanson Castle, the doctor a fellow kinsman he now considered a good friend. With the finishing touches almost complete to his face, he awaited the final transformation in his disguise.

The day before one of the lasses at the keep had trimmed his shoulder length hair to within a spiky inch from his scalp. She'd slapped on a thick black paste, let it sit for a while then told him to wash it out. He'd bent over a basin of flowing water, rinsed his hair then when he'd lifted his head and caught his reflection in one of the massive looking glasses of this time, his golden locks were gone. Midnight-black hair reigned. Miraculous.

This morn he'd even shaved his thick beard away, one he'd had for a good number of years, since the day it had first grown in at six and ten. He stroked over his jaw, the unusual smoothness of his shaven skin grating on him. "'Tis like I'm a lad again, Tavish."

"You'll get used to being without the beard, and it might pay for you not to catch a glimpse of yourself in the mirror just yet, particularly if you're having trouble adjusting to the changes. I've been able to knock a good decade off by removing every single wrinkle you had." Tavish set his instruments down

35

on the tray and pushed back on his padded stool with its wheels that rolled across the white tiled flooring.

Everything in Tavish's medical room was white, from the white-sheeted bed he sat on in the center of the room to the white painted walls, cupboard doors, and curtaining. The stainless steel benchtop was all that broke the clean color apart, and what an incredible benchtop it was. So finely crafted, and within those cupboards, well, Tavish had brought out so many new and astounding things that had aided him in his full healing this past month. Truly incredible.

This twenty-first century and all he'd discovered within it had both surprised and enthralled him. Although a recent trip into the village in one of their fast-moving wagons had near halted his heart from beating. An SUV Tavish had called it. Fully enclosed, the wagon of steel had sent them careening along a road of black tar with fierce speed. When he'd pressed a button and the window of sheer glass had rolled down, he'd half heaved over the side to find out where it had gone. Tavish had chuckled and hauled him back in.

Aye, if he could survive a journey in one of those speedy conveyances, he could certainly survive the change to his appearance. He nodded at his clansman. "I'd like to see what you've done. Make certain all is well."

"As you wish." Tavish pulled off his gloves, riffled through a drawer and pulled out a compact, flipped the cover open and exposed a looking glass tucked safely away inside. "I can't imagine anyone who met you at Carron Castle during your captivity will ever be able to identify you now. You've healed well this past month, your injuries all but gone, even the whip marks on your back."

"Och, hell." He almost dropped the compact. His lips looked as if bees had stung them, repeatedly, an enticing look on a lass for sure, but not on a hardened warrior. Every wrinkle he'd had around his eyes and forehead had vanished. It had taken him years to gather those marks of age. Gaping, he muttered, "What have you done, Tavish?"

"I've used Botox where needed. What it does is weakens the facial muscles so the wrinkles disappear, although it's temporary, the effects lasting about three to four months. I've also added some filler to your lips, and a touch to your cheekbones as well."

"Oh my." Annella walked in, her mouth wide open. "Is that you, Ronan?"

"Aye, scamp."

"You look"—she arched a brow as she wandered around him—"different. Very different."

"Will Duncan MacKenzie or his warriors see the real me through this disguise?" His younger sister would tell him the truth. She always had.

"Even I hardly recognize the real you." She stopped in front of him, cupped his cheeks and gently ran her fingers back and forth along his jaw. "Your skin is as smooth as a baby's bottom. I had no idea you could look so very handsome. No more beard for you."

"I liked my beard." He gritted his teeth, covered her hands with his then couldn't help but smile at his dearest kin. His sister, now a newlywed with a husband from this time who adored her beyond all reason, lived both here in the future and in the past. "Where's Alec?"

"My mate is training in the yard, as I too should be." Annella had grown up fighting right alongside him and Father, all three of them warriors through and through. In her black leather pants, billowy-sleeved blue tunic and sword gleaming at her hip, she popped a kiss on his forehead. "I shall miss you while you're gone. I expect you to find your mate and return with her, with all haste."

"I shall do exactly that, and at least I'm leaving you in the best of hands with Alec." He slid off the bed, his kilt brushing his knees as he clasped Tavish's forearm. "I thank you for all you've done. 'Tis a miracle you've worked for me."

"You're most welcome. You're free to leave whenever you please and track down your chosen one. There's no need for more checkups." Tavish grasped his forearm in return. "I wish you a safe journey and a most enjoyable hunt."

"I shall never cease chasing my chosen one, no matter how far she attempts to roam from me." He pulled on his billowy black tunic, tucked the hem under the belted waist of the MacKenzie tartan Annella had purchased for him from a store in the village. He grunted. Donning the enemy's colors grated on him, but he'd need to wear this plaid or else be discovered for who he truly was. At least he had a viable reason for arriving dressed as a MacKenzie warrior at Carron Castle. During his imprisonment, he'd learnt Coll was away on a mission to secure more warriors to his and Duncan's cause and he intended to offer his sword arm once he arrived. Men had been arriving daily at the keep during his imprisonment. Aye, he'd do whatever it took to claim Kyla, even pose as a MacKenzie.

"You're a Matheson, no matter what kilt you wear." Annella scooped his sword from the end of the medical bed and passed it to him. "Never forget that."

"Are you reading my mind again?"

"Dinnae I always?" She crossed her arms with a knowing smile. "You're also about to correct the wrong done to Kyla when she was but a child. Giving her back the choice so brutally taken from her is all that matters. She too is a Matheson, no' a MacKenzie. What name have you chosen for yourself?"

"Rand MacKenzie, from clan MacKenzie of Kintail." He'd thought long and hard about what name to select before the perfect one had come to him. As a lad of eight, he'd been busy carving "R and C" into the trunk of a pine tree overlooking the cliffs near the fae village when Christina had skipped up the trail and danced around him. With her golden-red curls bouncing about her shoulders and a mischievous smile on her face, she'd tapped the trunk before he'd finished inscribing the "C" for the first letter of her name and asked him what he'd been doing. His face had gotten all hot and he'd been unable to finish the inscription, had stopped at "*R and*" then stupidly babbled to her that *Rand* was a nickname.

She'd giggled and called him Rand for an entire week and he hadn't minded one bit, not since her happiness had brightened his heart. Even at the young age of eight, he'd known one day she would be his, but telling her then had been impossible. He'd kept the knowledge to himself, or at least he had until the day when he'd been imprisoned within the dungeons of Carron Castle and come face to face with her once more. For the past twenty years his wee Christina had been known as Kyla, and his very soul had ached for her and the loss she'd suffered.

Such a barrage of emotions had raced through him that day.

Even though cuffed and chained to the gritty dungeon wall, a rat scratching about within one darkened corner, he'd never been more in awe of the woman standing so magnificently before him. Those sweet curls of hers were even more thick and luscious than in her childhood, the color such a vibrant golden hue with strands of red woven in, her locks now swaying all the way to her bottom. The tiny freckles she'd had as a child still dusted her cheeks and as he'd looked into her eyes, he'd become lost within her stunning blue gaze. Shock and awe at finding her had swarmed him.

He'd been searching for her his entire life, had never given up the possibility of finding her, but learning the truth about her abduction had astounded him. Now, he intended on returning to the place of his imprisonment to claim her, to have her accept their bond and choose him the same way as he wished to choose her.

"I like that name. Rand is perfect." Annella hugged him. "Promise me you'll be careful during your hunt."

"Always, and I know I'll have you to contend with if I'm no'." Sword strapped on and his wrist daggers sheathed, he pulled on his boots.

"That's right." She squeezed his cheeks and sighed. "I shall miss this pretty face of yours while you're gone."

"If you call me pretty one more time I'll haul you over my knee and redden your backside with my belt." He wouldn't do such a thing, but hopefully the threat would hold.

"Liar, and I'd like to see you try with my chosen one so close." She pranced to the window overlooking the training yard below, shoved the window open and yelled, "Alec! I need my big bear to come and tussle with my bro—"

He was at the window in a flash, shoved a hand over his sister's mouth and muttered. "I dinnae need any bruises right now, scamp, no' until after I've successfully infiltrated Carron Castle." He truly needed to be away and not tussling with her mate yet again. Alec Matheson held one fierce ability, could battle as no other could. Still, he'd miss his sister terribly. He'd looked after her his entire life, didn't care to leave her behind but this coming mission was one he needed to embark on alone.

"What's your plan when you arrive at Carron?" Tavish shrugged his white coat off and hung it on a hook by the door.

"'Twill be impossible to lie to my mate. She'll learn the truth, just as soon as I can impart it."

"Good morn, everyone." Cherub swished into the room in a regal crimson gown with lace-edged sleeves, Kirk one step behind her in his kilt and leather jerkin. They'd both arrived a few hours ago, and after he'd laid out his plans for the day ahead, they'd offered to scout about Carron for him then report back with any findings.

"How did your search go?" He picked up his satchel where he'd propped it against the corner chair, hoisted it over his shoulder and crossed to Cherub.

"Very good. We arrived in time to catch Duncan riding out

with about half a dozen of his men. He returns to Ardan House, his keep a little farther along the loch from Carron Castle." Cherub touched his forehead then swished under his eyes. "Incredible. You've no wrinkles at all."

"You have no wrinkles yourself."

"Aye." A smile. "'Tis one of the benefits to being an immortal fae."

Kirk clutched his shoulder, his usual grin in place. "Welcome to the wrinkle-free club, my friend."

"Wrinkle-free? You say the strangest things." He couldn't help but chuckle at Kirk. He'd come to know the man well since he'd formed a mated bond with Cherub, respected and admired him for his dedication in joining their fae princess in her duty to her earthbound kind. "What of Kyla? Did you see her at all?"

"We did," Kirk answered him. "She left the keep with a guard and right now swims in a pool within the forest. Her guard hunts so she's alone. You can speak to her privately if you wish it."

"I more than wish it."

"Then we'll take you directly there." Cherub held out her arm to him. His people's princess held the time-walker ability and commanded the very *air* itself, could halt the wind or send it churning if she so desired. She could also cloak her form and become unseen to others, or if she wished, so too she could become as one with the very air itself and take on a mist form. The night of his escape from Carron's dungeons, Cherub had whipped up a mighty storm and unleashed it upon the warriors under Duncan's command. She would go to any length to ensure her people's survival, had certainly seen to his. "Take ahold of me and we'll be away."

"This I cannae wait for." He grasped her arm.

"Remember, no letting go." Kirk eyed him as he wrapped his arms around Cherub from behind. "If you do, you'll experience a far rougher journey than what is necessary."

"Thank you for the warning." Although he recalled his initial trip here to the twenty-first century with ease, even though he'd been badly beaten and whipped to within an inch of his life at the time.

"Good luck with the chase, and should you need me then call out." Annella blew him a kiss. "No one restrains my brother again and gets away with it." He didn't doubt she'd travel to him if she sensed he was in any danger at all.

"Aye, scamp, I'll make sure to pass that threat right along." He squeezed Cherub's arm. "'Tis time for me to confront my chosen one, to bring her around the mated way of thinking."

"That I wholeheartedly agree with. Let's tarry no more." Cherub twirled her fingers through the air and the wind rose and swirled all about.

A portal opened and he held onto Cherub as the three of them fell away into the churning abyss. Within the dark, lightning flashed and stars blazed. His soul lifted and his heart rejoiced at soon being closer to his chosen one once more. For the past month since his escape all he'd wished to do was heal so he might return to her. He longed to see the fiery spark in her blue eyes. She was spectacular, mesmerizing, a true Scottish lass with the fire of the fae in her blood. Aye, no more would he allow her to deny their bond.

"Here we are." Cherub settled them down and the churning darkness gave way to the vivid brightness of the day, the morning air crisp yet still holding the warmth of the sun. Blue skies reigned overhead with only the odd smattering of cloud, while pine and elm trees rose tall and strong. Birds chirped and flew from branch to branch.

"Kyla's about a hundred yards farther along this trail." Kirk gestured toward the scrub-lined pathway leading north. "I wish you well on your chase."

"Both of you have my immense thanks for all you've done." He stepped back. "Travel safely."

"We will, and be careful." The wind rushed and in the blink of the eye, Cherub disappeared with Kirk through another portal, the two gone just as quickly as they'd come.

Aye, 'twas time for him to be gone too.

Along the trail, he snuck then halted as up ahead splashing trickled toward him.

With nary a noise, he stepped out from amongst the thick trees encircling a clearing. Sunshine rippled across the glistening surface of a perfectly round pool holding his enticing siren within.

Scooping water at her sides, Kyla floated on her back, her waist-length locks splaying out like a lily pad of golden-red, her dainty face upturned and eyes closed. The water swelled around her, cascaded over her bare legs and belly. Her full breasts rose above the surface and her rosy nipples sat stiff and pointy on top. Hell. He hadn't expected to find her without a stitch of clothing on.

He should turn away, give her the privacy she desired, only doing so right now was impossible. Her lips, softly parted, drew his gaze even though every curved inch of her remained on glorious display. He wanted to kiss her, to know her taste and touch, just as he'd desired the same during his captivity.

Memories surged, of the moment when he'd sensed the depth of their bond taking form and the strands between their souls weaving more firmly together. Deep underground behind iron bars, he'd yanked on his cuffed hands chained back against the wall, while she'd stood on the other side of his cell in the darkened passageway with a guard at her side.

"*Stand aside, Gordon.*" Kyla had swished into the cell after Gordon had unlocked it, a bowl of steaming stew and a tankard of water in hand. In a sleeveless teal gown and a cream under-tunic, a heavy silver-chained girdle clasped around her tiny waist, she'd scraped a wooden crate from the corner forward and set the food and drink on top of it.

He hadn't been able to get his fill of her, his gaze devouring his chosen one as he'd searched to ensure she remained unharmed since their first meeting the day before. That had been when he'd learned her new name. Known as Kyla, the Chief of MacKenzie's foster daughter, she'd lived within his enemy's household since her abduction and had arrived here recently to visit her two favored foster brothers.

"*Are you well, Kyla?*" His voice had been a mess as he'd spoken to her, all raspy and dry.

"*You need never fear for me, Ronan. I am amongst my own kin here.*" She shot a look at Gordon. "*Leave. He willnae eat with you present.*"

"*You pander to him and shouldnae. I shall give you five minutes and no more.*" Gordon had snorted as he'd walked out the door, closed it after himself with a loud clang and marched down the corridor.

"*You must eat and drink if you wish to maintain your strength.*" She'd picked up the chipped tankard she'd brought and held it up to his chapped lips. "*Now, afore I am forced to leave and you miss the chance to do so.*"

"*Cease using force against me.*" He'd taken a hearty swallow of the water. She'd unknowingly used force, her fae mind-walker skill rising as she'd issued her command, her mind naturally seeking out his due to their bond. "*I can sense your fae skill, your subtle yet clear push within my mind to make me obey your orders.*"

"*I have no idea what you speak of. I hold no fae skill. I am a MacKenzie, the foster daughter of my chief, a fact you'd best no' forget.*"

"*Trust me, you hold a fae skill whether you wish to acknowledge it or no', although it likely lays buried somewhat inside you since you have no' had the chance to be guided by our people in the full use of it. You can do more than touch another's mind. You can also delve deeper and sway our thoughts. I too am part fae and can sense your ability."*

She'd touched her head, confusion swirling within her gaze.

"Listen to me well, Kyla. Twenty years ago a young lass was taken from the fae village farther along the loch from the House of Clan Matheson. Her name was Christina and she was the first and only child born to Isaiah and Grace. In the middle of the night, under the cover of darkness, she disappeared without a trace. Kidnapped, the elders of the village said, although they couldnae find her, and no one had demanded coin for her return. I remember the lass well even though I was only a lad of eight at the time. The wee one always intrigued me with her mass of golden-red curls and blue eyes."

"I cannae possibly be this lass you speak of." With an obstinate shake of her head, she'd dipped the spoon into the stew, held the mouthful to his lips, her beautiful blue eyes narrowed with frustration and anger. *"I know who my kin are, and 'tis no clan Matheson. Eat. Now."*

"You're doing it again, using your skill against me. Touch your mind to mine with more strength then issue the command you wish obeyed. It'll force me to your hand far faster than how you are currently making your demands."

"All right. I can touch my mind to another's, have always known I could, but I've never forced another to my will, and no one has ever discovered my touch within their mind, other than those whom I trust. I've always taken every precaution. I didnae mean to touch your mind, did so afore I could help myself. Please, you must promise me that you'll never tell another soul of what I've done. My parents' lives depend on it." She'd prodded the spoon against his closed lips once more. *"Open your mouth. I wish for you to eat. You need the nourishment, and to maintain your strength."*

"You'll learn soon enough how to use your skill to its full force if you but return to your true people. Only those of fae blood can in truth sense your touch. You can never hide that

from those of your own kind." He'd opened his mouth and slurped the stew down. "*Even as young as Christina was when she was taken, her very soul cried out to mine. I knew we were mated, even though so few do at such a young age.*"

He'd never joined with another from their clan, always sensed a restlessness within him for the one woman being held far beyond his reach. He'd known she awaited him somewhere, that she would remain lost to him until he'd found her. Now that he had, he'd never allow her to be snatched away from him again. She needed him, as much as he needed her.

"*I said open your mouth.*" Kyla jammed another spoonful of stew between his lips.

"*Look inside your heart and tell me you dinnae feel something toward me.*"

"*I feel plenty, including frustration and annoyance.*" She'd continued to feed him, not allowing him another moment to speak until the bowl was empty and the spoon clattered against the base. "*Now, when the guard brings you a meal, you'll eat it.*"

"*Come closer, Kyla.*"

"*I certainly willnae.*" She'd slammed her hands on her hips.

"*Aye, you will.*" He'd hooked one leg around the back of her legs and she'd toppled forward, palms flattened against his chest and her breath whooshing out.

"*You have no right to touch me, Ronan Matheson.*"

"*I have every right.*" Unable to help himself, he'd buried his nose in her hair. "*It feels so good to have you so close, to have your hands upon me. Many of our fae-blooded kind are soul bound to another, and when they come of age and find their chosen ones, they join together in all ways, the silken strands between their souls weaving together into one.*"

"*I sense naught between us.*" She'd squeezed her eyes shut then pushed herself away from him, straightened her shoulders and glared. "*You are my brother's prisoner and he intends to use you to ensure your father's compliance. We need Niall Matheson*" *on our side.*" She'd brushed her teal skirts, collected the bowl and tankard and swished to the cell door.

"*Where is my father being kept?*" He'd pushed forward, his chains rattling.

"*Somewhere safe. You must no' fear for him.*" She'd left, taking his heart with her when she had.

His chosen one had been raised far away from her true clan, and now his battle to capture and contain his fiery mate had begun, a battle he'd never walk away from.

Today, she'd learn that the fae never gave up on one of their own.

He lowered his satchel to the ground, toed off his boots and unbelted his sword. 'Twas time for his mate to see he was back and wasn't leaving without her, not one more time. At the edge of the pool, he planted his hands on his hips, determination spurring him on. "Kyla."

Water splashed and his enticing siren gasped and dunked under the surface. She came back up spluttering, her beautiful blue eyes alight. "Coll? What are you—" She scrubbed her knuckles into her eyes then blinked. "Nay, you're no' Coll. Who are you?"

"Rand MacKenzie, my lady, at your service."

"Then be gone if you wish to be of service to me."

"That is an impossible request." He unraveled the MacKenzie plaid he'd donned, dropped it onto the ground next to her belongings and in his black tunic covering him to mid-thigh, walked along the mossy edge of the pool toward the overhanging ledge at the far side. He scooped up her shift lying on the stone and lifted his gaze to his chosen one. "Why did you call me Coll?"

"You look so similar to my foster brother, shockingly so." She treaded water, the murky depths thankfully now hiding her body from him. Certainly if he caught sight of her bare skin again, he'd want only to hold her in his arms. "How did you sneak past my guard, Rand MacKenzie?"

"I arrived through one of Cherub's portals." The truth. He had no reason to lie to her, not when he wanted her to know exactly who he was. "You've surely heard of the fae princess who is the guardian of the fae?"

"I—I—" She gasped and went down again before bobbing back to the surface. She spluttered, shoved her wet hair back from her face. "I have, but—who exactly are you?"

"Deep in your soul, you know exactly who I am." Needing to be closer, he dove and kicked through the darkened depths toward the one woman who belonged to him, just as much as he belonged to her.

'Twas time to confront his chosen one, to chase her until she succumbed to his desires. He would entice and woo her, hunt and claim the one who held the other half of his soul.

No more would he delay.

Chapter 2

Kyla screeched as the dark-haired warrior known as Rand dove into the pool. He burst from the depths and treaded water in front of her, his stunning golden eyes shining bright. She could drown in that heavenly gaze, would never mistake it for another's.

Memories surged, the name "Rand" echoing through her mind. She'd been so young, had skipped up the cliff side trail near their village and found Ronan at the top beside a pine tree, his dirk in hand. She'd danced around him, caught the word *Rand* etched into the trunk and asked him what he'd been doing. He'd gone all flush-faced, muttered something about it being a nickname and she'd giggled and teased him all week about it.

Deep in your soul, you know exactly who I am.

His words taunted her.

Gone was his usual head of shoulder-length locks and scruffy beard. The stunning golden color had shimmered bright even under the meager candlelight within the dungeons. Now, dark hair graced his head and somehow the wrinkles beside his eyes and across his forehead had disappeared. His cheeks appeared a little higher, and his mouth was most definitely fuller. "How is it you're here?"

"Say my name." Such need flared in his gaze.

"Ronan." Gently, she touched her palm to his cheek, her very soul soaring free.

"Aye, you'll always recognize me, no matter if I try to conceal my true identity."

"What are you doing here?"

"That should be obvious." He held out her wet shift. "Does my lady wish her undergarment returned?"

"Aye, but your lady also wishes you'd never returned." She snatched her shift from him, tried to find the hem within the drenched mess and only ended up sinking under the surface once more.

He grasped her hips and lifted her back up. "Here, allow me to aid you."

"How did you manage to change your appearance so greatly?" She slung one arm around his neck and frowned at his plump lips. "Those should be considered criminal."

"'Tis my disguise so I might infiltrate Carron Castle without issue, and you should be asking me why I stayed away for so long."

"You arena permitted near Coll's keep, and this pool is far too close to it for my liking." He'd shaved off his thick beard, his firm and angular jaw so enticing. She smoothed along his chin and down the long line of his neck to the deep V in his black tunic. The fabric clung to him, outlined the wide expanse of his muscled chest and—oh dear. She snatched her hand away. "Have you fully healed?"

"Aye, and those who are soul bound need the touch of their chosen one. I can no more release you than you can truly pull away."

"Soul bound we might be, but enemies we still are."

"You'll never be my enemy, Kyla. You're Isaiah and Grace's daughter, a mind-walker and one of the fae. Even afore you were kidnapped, I knew you'd one day be mine. Since I've been gone all I've wished to do is return so I might hold you in my arms again. I'm certainly prepared for any battle to claim you." His golden gaze swirled and when she touched her mind to his, his thoughts barreled through with such fierce intensity. He wasn't leaving, not without her.

"Where have you been this past month?" So many times she'd tried to reach him, to touch her mind to his only each time she'd came up against a black hole of nothingness. "You said you arrived through one of Cherub's portals."

"Aye, our fae princess, following my rescue from Carron's dungeons, took me to a place far beyond these lands, to Ivanson Castle in the twenty-first century."

"I've yet to meet Cherub, but she and my foster father have battled many a time. I did though see her that night you escaped. I watched from my chamber window as she stood within the inner bailey and whipped up a storm that kept our warriors away from the dungeon's entrance. She truly took you to the future?"

"She did, and once there, I was attended to by a healer, a great physician who also aided me in my physical transformation. Things are so different in that time. Medical advances have been made, progress which boggles the mind." He lowered his gaze and swept it over her lips then lower still, down her neck before he gulped, his throat working hard. "You need to don your shift. I cannae quite see below the water's surface, but I know what's there all the same. I watched you from the trees afore I made my presence known."

She should be embarrassed, particularly with the way he now held her, but that emotion didn't arise. Being with her chosen one filled her with such need, far beyond anything else. "Hold onto me while I put it on."

"Of course." His grip on her waist tightened.

"Thank you." She shimmied the clingy cotton over her head and pulled it down before clutching his broad shoulders. "When you were last here you asked about your father and I couldnae answer you as I wished to. Niall's well and his bond with Muirin deepens. Duncan rode out this morn to Ardan House to check on his training."

"I didnae care for the underhanded way Muirin ensured my father's capture and mine, yet I understand why she did so." He curled his fingers into her hips. "They're soul bound, and none should ever separate those who are. That goes for us as well. I want my chosen one, have waited far too long to join us together in all ways." He swam with her back toward the bank, lifted her up onto the mossy edge then heaved himself up beside her. Water sluiced down his body, plastering his tunic to his chest and thighs.

"Sometimes things go beyond our control."

"As they have for us." He picked up her hand, gently uncurled her fingers and spread her palm against his chest, right over the pounding beat of his heart.

"I love Duncan and Coll. They were my lifeline after my abduction, have looked after me each and every day since." She caressed his chest, her fingers playing with the loosened ties at the V of his tunic.

"I'm glad you had them, but now you also have me." He tipped her back onto the lush moss and laid down half over top of her.

"Ronan." She should push him away, only this might be the only opportunity she ever had to experience a few moments of his touch, a sliver of time she desperately desired afore she spoke vows with Duncan. "There's something I need to tell you."

"Allow our bond to strengthen." He pulled her onto her side so she faced him, smoothed one hand along her outer thigh and tucked her top leg snugly between his bare legs, their bodies aligned from head to toe. "Give me some time to show you how deep it can run. Touch me, just as I wish to touch you."

Mated pairs needed the touch of their chosen one on a deeper level to anything else. Before she'd been taken from the village, she'd touched the minds of her fae-blooded kind who were mated, had sensed the deep love that drove them within their bonds. If possible, she would touch him just as freely as she desired, but—

"I've longed to hold you in my arms, Kyla. Doing so calms and soothes me in a way I can never explain." He skimmed one finger along her shift's wet and clingy neckline, right where the top edge sagged and exposed the upper swells of her breasts. "Although if I go too far in touching you, tell me, but I'm thirsty for more, want only to surround myself with you and all that you are."

"I shouldnae be encouraging your pursuit." Except she couldn't help but hold onto him too. She was so starved for his touch.

"I will pursue you to the ends of this Earth, shall never give you up." His gaze raked over her, burning hot and soul tingling as he followed the curves of her breasts and her hips under her wet shift.

"Colin MacKenzie has controlled my actions since my abduction and always will."

"He controls naught if you cease giving him the power to do so. Touch my mind, see for yourself how committed I am to the path I've now chosen, a path that will only ever lead to you." He caught her cheeks, smoothed his thumbs across her lips, his breath stuttering as he leaned in and pressed his forehead against hers. "Accept me. Choose me, the same way I wish to choose you. Allow me to honor and cherish you, for the rest of our days."

A gentle breeze whispered through the trees and swirled over them, fluttered his tunic's drying hem and gave a glimpse of his muscled thigh. She squeezed her eyes shut, opened them again and almost melted at the intoxicating heat in his golden eyes. Like liquid fire, his gaze blazed strong and true. "Kiss me, Ronan. Please."

"I've longed to hear you say that." He captured her mouth with his and licked across her tongue, his breath mingling so seductively with hers and making her arch into him for more.

Gently, she sucked on his indecently full lower lip then indulged in her need for even more. Fingers digging into his shoulders, she kissed him back, so wantonly before she pulled him fully on top of her and sighed as his heavenly weight settled exactly where she needed it. Reveling in his hot and virile scent, the sun overhead rising higher and bathing them in its warmth, she embraced her mate and the depth of their bond. "I like your kisses, my stubborn mate."

"Aye, I can be beyond stubborn when my course is set, and currently my course is set on you."

"So I see, yet you've returned for me when you shouldnae have."

"I would never have been able to stay away from you." He kissed her again and she held on, grasped a firm hold of his mind and tunneled deep inside.

"What did I do to deserve you, Ronan?" She would crave him for the rest of her days, her heart clenching at the thought of ever having to let him go. This was pure torture and denying him was impossible.

"You're everything I could ever desire in a mate, all I've ever hoped for, a woman of strength, loyalty and passion. I adore and respect that you stand so strongly at your foster brothers' sides, but now 'tis time for you to stand just as strongly at mine." He palmed the back of her head and held her mouth to within a breath of his lips. "You are my destiny and have been since the moment of your birth, just as I will always be yours."

He swooped in and took her breath away with his fierce passion and powerfully spoken words.

Aye, he was her destiny, except how did she go about making everything right? How could she protect her parents from Colin if she chose Ronan over Duncan? Never had she been placed in such a difficult position before.

* * * *

With all the longing he held deep inside him, Ronan allowed his desire for Kyla its full release. He rolled them both until she came up over top of him, caressed down her sides and roamed over her lush bottom. Hands bunched in her wet undergarment, he scrunched the long length of it up and smoothed over the backs of her legs. Her fast breathing and racing heartbeat had his passion flaring. He took her mouth with his and kissed her, deeply, until her sweet and alluring fragrance wrapped around him and saturated his senses. Since the moment he'd found her in the dungeons, she'd tempted him beyond his endurance and he didn't doubt she always would.

"Mmm, Ronan." She murmured his name against his lips then kissed him with such soul-searing passion in return. "I have so much to tell you."

"I want to touch you, as freely as those who are mated do." All that roared through his mind was the need to mate, to bind his chosen one to him in the most elemental way. "Will you allow it?"

"Allow what, exactly?" She nuzzled his neck, licked over his thumping pulse point then hands on his chest, pushed up and straddled him, her legs either side of his thighs and her shift stretched tight across her knees. Her damp golden-red locks cascaded down her back and swept across his legs behind her.

"Allow me to bring you pleasure, to tighten the bonds between us." Slowly, he slid his hands along her upper thighs toward the heat of her pressed against him, her shift rising inch by inch as he did and his need for her an unstoppable beat in his blood. "I'll take naught from you, will leave you fully intact, but I want to love you right here and right now, with all that I am."

"I can barely think straight." She wriggled against him and his cock hardened painfully.

"Then allow me to do the thinking for both of us." He

needed to touch her, all of her, to show her how it should be between a mated pair. He eased one hand underneath the fabric of her shift, the cotton sliding cool and wet across the back of his hand. He couldn't halt his current desire, didn't have a chance of doing so. All he wanted to do was push his fingers deep inside her, to give her whatever pleasure he could, to hear her scream his name and know she did so because of him.

"Aye, touch me." She licked her lips, slowly leaned in, her breasts swaying forward and he lifted one clear of the sagging neckline and flicked his thumb over the beaded tip.

He palmed her full breast, squeezed the lush flesh and with her mind embedded deep within his mind, he showed her through his thoughts exactly how he wanted her to lean forward and put her breast in his mouth.

"I see you are going to be a very demanding mate. Stubborn times two." She leaned forward then gasped as he suctioned his mouth around her delectable nipple. He played the tip with his tongue, drew the bud deep inside his mouth and wished only to consume her. She tasted exquisite, her skin cool from the water but also flaring with heat from his touch and she clung to him, pushed the sweet morsel even deeper into his mouth before arching her back and rocking her lower body over him.

His blood roared for more and he couldn't halt his need. He freed her other breast then gave it as much attention as he'd laved on the first.

"Mmm, so divine." She cupped the back of his head, her fingers spearing through his hair as she held his mouth against her. "I need to touch you too. Show me what you want me to do within your mind."

He gave her the image, of her hand wrapping around his aching shaft, of how he wanted her to stroke him and she shuffled back a touch, lifted his shirt hem and wrapped her hand around his erection. No hesitation. She touched him as if she owned him, which she did. All of him. Such a kaleidoscope of emotions roared through him, from pleasure to pain and everything in between. "I'm going to touch you below as well, Kyla. I promise to be careful."

"I trust you."

"Aye, as those who are mated do." He nudged her legs a little farther apart, the heady aroma of her arousal swirling around him. Along her hot inner folds, he stroked, back and forth until he slid one finger deep inside her channel.

"Oh, that feels exquisite." She captured his mouth and kissed him, her lips moving over his in the most divine way.

Hell, his woman certainly knew how to kiss, to stoke the fire deep inside him into raging life. All he wanted to do right now was toss her onto her back, dive between her legs and imbibe at the very heart of her. Instead, he plunged a second finger inside her and caressed her in time with how she stroked him. She was his sustenance, the only woman who would own him, heart, body and soul and he never wanted this moment to end.

Fondling her deep inside, he allowed his hunger for her to roar to life and as he did, she swiped her thumb over the head of his cock, made a buzz of sensations fire up at the base of his spine and sizzle around to the front. His cock wept for more and he pushed deeper into her incredible touch. "Dinnae stop what you're doing to me." He seized her mouth, swept his tongue into the hot cavern and tasted the incredible honeyed recesses within. "I want a lifetime with you, beginning right now, Kyla."

"I can see everything you wish for me to do within your mind and I hope I'm getting it right." She pumped his shaft, gently cupped his balls with her other hand and he gritted his teeth to keep from coming. Nay, he wouldn't allow his passion its release until he'd wrung hers from her as well.

He drove his fingers into her, tapped a spot that made her cry out with pleasure then whimper for even more as she heaved her breasts harder against his chest. With one more flick of his thumb over her nub, she exploded, her inner core dragging his fingers ever deeper inside her as she came, over and over.

No longer could he hold back. As she pumped him, he let go and fire shot through him, his essence spurting free in one fast burn.

His seed coated her fingers and he roared his pleasure, the silken strands of their mated bond weaving even more fully together. Panting against her lips, he murmured, "Marry me, Kyla. Be my wife."

* * * *

Kyla slumped on top of Ronan, pure pleasure still racing through her body and his request for marriage resounding in her head. When his cock had pulsed in her hand, his essence had streamed so hot and thick from him and her inner channel had sucked greedily at his fingers. This was passion, what she'd never have with Duncan, never wanted to have with any other than him. How she wanted her chosen one to simply take her away from this place so she no longer had to think, only that was impossible. Touching her forehead against his, she gave a little shake of her head. "I cannae marry you, no' when my parents' safety will come into question. I fear for them, greatly."

"Tell me why. Your papa holds the battle skill and your mama the ability to foresee another's death. They are strong in their own rights, are safe and well."

"Should I choose you, then they will forfeit their lives." She flopped onto her back on the mossy ground beside him. She'd loved each and every one of his kisses and even though they hadn't joined in the way of man and wife, in that moment when his seed had rushed forth from him, she'd desperately wished that his essence had instead spurted deep inside her. "I've been protecting them my entire life. They are why I've never left the MacKenzie's keep. I've never even attempted to make contact with them."

"Explain everything to me." He edged up onto his side,

stroked one hand down her arm and looked into her eyes. "You're carrying a burden you've no need to."

"The day I was abducted by Colin MacKenzie, he decreed that one day I'd wed one of his three sons, that he wished for my fae blood to flow strongly through his line. He also warned me that should I ever defy him then he'd ensure my parents' death. He knows naught of my skill, has never told another of my fae blood in case my parents hear of it."

"I can warn your parents of his threat, ensure they're kept safe behind the fortified walls of the House of Clan Matheson rather than at the village. Your mama will know if any harm is about to befall either your papa or herself. That is the beauty of her skill. She can keep them both safe if you but allow it." He stroked a finger under her chin and down the long column of her neck. "You arenae a child anymore. 'Tis time for you to live, to bind yourself to me and to learn all about your true clan."

"Colin always keeps his word." Hot tears burned behind her eyes. "He'll hurt them."

Determination flared in his gaze. "I'll make certain your parents take every precaution."

"There is more."

"Tell me. Whatever fears you have I'll aid you in overcoming them."

"Duncan and I are betrothed. We're to speak vows when he returns from Ardan House in a few days' time." She couldn't halt the scorching stream of hot tears from flowing down her cheeks. "I've made such a mess of things. I truly couldnae see past the threat to my parents' lives, regardless of their fae abilities. If I could be taken from them, then they surely could be too."

"I understand, and you've done all you could these past twenty years, what you believed would be best. No' only will I speak to your parents, but I'll also speak with Duncan about your betrothal and explain the turn of events. I'll certainly never allow you to wed him, no' while there's still breath in my body. I will fight for you." Firm words, and as she delved deeper within his mind, she saw the absolute truth of them. He'd never let her go, not now he'd finally found her.

"Both Coll and Duncan have known who I was from the very beginning. A few days afore my abduction, Mama took me to Colin's stronghold after receiving a vision about his sons. She feared for them and though I cannae explain why, 'tis the truth. I trust them, and neither have ever raised arms against a Matheson and never shall. That I give you my word on."

"I can see how great your love is for them, but 'tis you and I who are soul bound." He rose to his feet and pulled her to hers, lifted her fingers to his lips and kissed each one. "I'll make things right, go and see Duncan and speak to him of our bond."

"You make everything sound so simple. What if it isnae? What if my parents are harmed, and all because I chose you over Duncan? I would never be able to live with myself if it all went terribly wrong."

"We cannae control other people's actions, only our own. All I ask is that you take a leap of faith and accept my aid. Dinnae give up the good fight, for I know your parents never would. Come, let's wash up so we can dress and leave. I have much to do to secure your hand in marriage, which now includes breaking your betrothal to another and ensuring your parents are kept safe." He leaned over the side of the pool, scooped water and splashed himself clean.

"I want to come with you when you leave to see Duncan." She cleaned herself, righted her shift.

"War rages at present. How often do you ride for Ardan?" He set a hand at her back and steered her around the pool toward their belongings, picked up his plaid and wrapped it around her.

"Duncan has become fiercely overprotective of late. I'm permitted to come this far from the keep since we have guards positioned along the main trail routes, but—" Oh, she'd clear forgotten. "Gordon came with me this day and hunts nearby. He'll be awaiting my call so we can return."

"I'll deal with Gordon." He caught her hand, pressed it against his thumping heartbeat. "My disguise is in place and he will know me only as Rand MacKenzie until I've spoken with your brother. I'll never allow another to toss me back into your dungeons and keep me away from you."

She spread her hand over his wet tunic, the fabric clinging to his muscled body and displaying every deliciously sculptured plane. Sweeping downward, she stroked over his rigid abs which tightened under her touch. Her mate was an elixir of the most decadent sort, one she would crave for the rest of her life and of that she had no doubt. She'd take this chance given to her, to try and claim back all she'd ever lost. "You're mine."

"Aye, as you're mine." He slowly lowered to one knee, brought her hand to his mouth and pressed his lips against her palm. "I have something I must say to you, and to do so afore we return to Coll's keep."

"You do?"

"Aye. From this day forth I give you my oath, Kyla. With my body and all that I am, I will honor you. I wish to give you my name, for my clan to be yours, for us to live as man and wife. I give you my word I'll keep you safe, honor your needs and desires above my own, watch over your nearest and dearest as well." He looked deep into her eyes. "This day I give you my full and complete protection. You hold the other half of my soul, and never will I release you to another."

A slow heat invaded her limbs, a rippling wave of warmth that spread through her body. No one had ever declared such an oath to her. She sank to her knees, his words touching her very heart and soul. "I too would like to give you my oath. With my body and all that I am, I will honor your needs above my own, accept your full and complete protection. I hold the other half of your soul, and I will never release it to another. I wish to place my trust in you, to no longer give Colin any control over me."

"You do me the greatest honor with such an oath." He slid one hand around the back of her head, his fingers spearing through her damp tresses as he leaned in, his lips a whisper from hers.

"Ronan Matheson!" Gordon stormed out from behind a tree, and her heart almost catapulted from her chest. "Your disguise certainly would have fooled me had you no' just admitted to the truth. I shall never allow you anywhere near my lady. She is betrothed to my laird, no other oaths permitted. You clearly wish to go to war with us."

"You misunderstand. I am here only to claim my chosen one." Ronan pushed her in behind him, shielding her with his body just as Gordon slid his sword free from its sheath.

"I've misunderstood naught." Gordon charged forward and Ronan snatched his sword from his pile of belongings on the ground and slammed his blade into Gordon's.

Their weapons clashed and steel rang loud against steel.

Gordon heaved back and thrust again.

Ronan blocked Gordon's next swift blow. "Put your weapon down, man. You could too easily harm Kyla."

"Leave this place now and I'll ensure she comes to no harm." Gordon's gaze glinted with loathing. "You have no right to be here on MacKenzie land."

"Nay, this madness must stop." She rushed forward and Ronan blocked her, pushed her back.

"Clearly you wish to revisit your cell." Gordon attacked and Ronan ducked his swift strike, whirled around and swiped his blade across Gordon's chest, metal scraping over metal.

"My next strike will be where you'll bleed. Make no mistake." Ronan dropped low, swept his leg out and kicked Gordon across his knees.

Toppling, Gordon hauled his dagger free, went to throw it but he slammed to the ground and hit his head on a protruding rock. Skin split open and blood gushed forth, his dagger embedded in his own wrist from the fall.

"Damn it." Ronan scanned the trees, hunkered down and pressed two fingers to Gordon's neck. "His heart still beats, albeit slow and unsteady."

"You should've allowed me to explain things to him." She dropped down beside him. "Gordon wouldnae have raised his sword against you if I had. Duncan allows none within his ranks to harm one of the fae, a stipulation all have agreed to, including Gordon and even though he does no' hold a great deal of love for your clan, he still abides by Duncan's decree. Even the two guards who flayed you have been sent far away."

"Gordon barely gave me the chance to speak, let alone you." He tore a strip from the hem of his black tunic and wrapped the cloth around Gordon's head, tore another length off, pulled Gordon's dagger from his wrist and bound the deep wound. "He'll need stitches or else he'll bleed out. I shouldnae have forgotten he remained so close by. Cherub and Kirk warned me you had a guard and it clear slipped my mind."

"I'll stitch his wounds the moment we return to the keep." She'd been cavorting with her mate when an entire garrison of highly trained warriors remained so very close by. "This is all my fault. Gordon's allegiance belongs to Duncan and he knew of my betrothal, clearly considered you a direct threat when he heard our oaths. Until you speak to Duncan, you must no' tell another exactly who you are."

"I agree. I'll remain as Rand."

Blood leaked through the cloth wrapped around Gordon's wrist and she tore a strip from her shift and bound another layer of cotton around it. Good. The flow eased with the added pressure and no longer stained the cloth. She lifted Gordon's closed eyelids, the whites of his eyes showing and a massive bruise blooming on his forehead. "He is out to it, well and truly."

"Let's dress. We need to return, immediately." He aided her

to her feet and gripped her shoulders. "Gordon's presence here causes an issue, but no' an irreversible one. We'll return to the keep and once we have, you tend his wounds while I ride for Ardan. 'Twill be the quickest way to see my conversation with Duncan done. Is Coll still on his mission, as he was during my imprisonment?"

"Aye, he still scours the length and breadth of MacKenzie land in his call-to-arms. He wishes for men to join him, who will remain both loyal to him and hold sympathy for your clan."

"Sympathy for my Matheson kin?"

"Aye, and please dinnae ask me anymore about that." She wrung the water from her shift, flapped out her gown and pulled it over her head. Layers of midnight-blue velvet shimmered down to her ankles and she laced the front stays, belted her girdle at her waist and stuffed her feet into her slippers.

Ronan dressed beside her, belted his kilt, stripped his wet tunic off and donned a dry one from his bag before strapping his weapons on. He grasped Gordon, hefted the man up and over his shoulder then eyed the trail ahead. "Lead the way, my bride-to-be."

Oh, what a dream that would be. She held his words close to her heart as she stuffed her belongings in her bag, snatched up Ronan's satchel then dashed along the forest trail toward Carron. The wind rose as she made the quick trek back and once she broke free of the woods, the formidable stone walls of the keep rose high ahead. She hurried toward the postern gate where armed guards patrolled the battlements above.

"Kyla!" Hamish, Duncan's closest confidant, a man who knew the truth about her and her brothers' fae blood, lifted a hand. "Is that Coll with you?"

"Nay, 'tis Rand MacKenzie." Over her shoulder, she whispered to Ronan, "Hamish is Muirin's brother and one of the full-blooded fae. He also holds 'the sight' and receives visions when harm is about befall us. He's been instrumental in ensuring all has gone well of late, his knowledge immense, the same as Muirin's is. We should tell him the truth, allow him to aid you in your plight. He would never harm a Matheson."

"No' yet. I wish to see for myself that I can trust him. I willnae risk losing you a second time because I didnae take all care." He waved out. "I'm told your name is Hamish. I stumbled upon the lady and this warrior in the forest. Unfortunately, he's injured himself and needs tending. I ask to be granted access to Carron's keep."

"Wait right there." Hamish disappeared from the battlements and tramped down the stairwell, appeared below and shoved the postern gate open. He cast his gaze over Gordon's slumped form. "How did all this happen?"

"Allow me to explain." She snuck in front of Ronan since he'd moved to place himself between her and Hamish. "Gordon, ah, tripped and fell, hit his head on a rock, and…" How did she explain his wrist wound? "Stabbed himself when he did, accidentally, of course."

"I've never known the man to be so clumsy." Hamish shook his head. "All these injuries came at his own hand?"

"Aye, Gordon had a wee bit too much to drink last eve." She motioned to Ronan. "I've met Rand afore, during a clan gathering. He's an honorable warrior, heard of Coll's call-to-arms and traveled here to offer his sword arm. I've informed him that Duncan is at Ardan House and he would need to visit him there if he wished to speak to him afore joining our cause."

"I didnae 'see' Rand's coming arrival."

"That would be because he means us no harm. Surely you wouldnae have 'seen' something unless he did, correct?" She held her breath, prayed fervently her word would stand.

"Aye, you're correct." Hamish cocked a brow at Ronan. "Where exactly do you hail from, Rand?"

"A village to the south of Kintail, and all is as the lady has explained. I've come to offer my sword arm, would like to speak to Duncan first to ensure his approval if I might?" He slipped in front of her again. Aye, definitely stubborn times two.

"Might we go inside?" She ducked around Ronan once more then with her back to him, stamped on top of his booted feet to keep him in place, all while smiling cheerily at Hamish. Let her chosen one try to whip in front of her now. Goodness. The males in the mated bond were notoriously overprotective, and her mate appeared no different even though she stood within a stone's throw of a garrison of warriors who'd protect her with their very lives. He was one man against so many until he'd spoken to Duncan and fixed everything she'd set moving on the wrong path. Drat it all. If only he'd arrived yesterday. Her betrothal would be one less thing he'd have to fix.

"Aye, come inside." Hamish stepped aside and gestured for her and Ronan to proceed him through the gate. "Never have I looked more forward to a vision as I do right now."

"As I look forward to you receiving one too." She desperately looked forward to it. Hamish could be trusted, implicitly.

Chapter 3

"This way, Rand." Kyla dashed across the inner courtyard toward the front doors of the keep, halted in the entryway and motioned for him to go up the side stairs so they could divert the great hall and those who would have already assembled there for the midday meal. At least she'd gotten her chosen one safely inside the keep without issue. Now to get him back out again and on his way to Ardan, and preferably with Hamish at his side. The seer would watch over him, his fae blood demanding he keep his own people safe. "Rand, take the first chamber on your right once you reach the first landing."

"Will do."

"You may have already secured the lady's trust, but you've yet to secure mine." Hamish pounded upstairs after Ronan and she chased them both.

"I came upon the lady by chance and I only sought to ensure she came to no harm, to return her safely to Carron and of course that her guardsman receives the care he needs." Ronan swept inside the chamber she'd indicated, carefully eased Gordon over his shoulder and laid him down on the sheeted bed.

"Clearly Gordon is unable to give me an account from his own mouth." Hamish moved to the other side of the bed and lifted Gordon's closed eyelids. "Accidents happen, of course, but he is badly hurt."

"His was a most unfortunate accident." She set her bag and Ronan's down in the corner, closed the door then crossed to the side table before the unlit fireplace where she kept her herbs and healing supplies. "I'll have Gordon back on his feet in no time."

She searched for the plantain she'd gathered from the forest only a few days ago. Various herbs still hung on a wire near the open window and from amongst the bunches, she plucked what she needed. She tore the leaves from the stem and along with a stone mortar and pestle, mashed and ground the plantain herb into a green paste, a salve she used for cleansing wounds and preventing them from festering. "Hamish, I need you to light the fire and set the pot of water to boiling."

With a frown at Ronan, Hamish knelt at the hearth, pulled the stringy bark off of a log, struck flint with his dirk and coaxed the sparks to life. He added twigs and wood until the flames rose high then set the blackened pot of water over top.

"What do you need of me?" Ronan brushed in behind her as she stood at Gordon's bedside, his hand smoothing discretely down her back.

"Remove Gordon's boots and chainmail. When he awakens, I want him as comfortable as possible." She delved deeper within Ronan's mind and began to fuse a stronger link between them. Filaments of gold spun thicker as she created a merged link of the mind, one that would allow her to go beyond just reading his thoughts to speaking to him mind to mind, a link she'd only ever created with one other when her ability had strengthened enough to do so. Ten years of age she'd been, her friendship with Fiona steadfast and sure. Along the golden strands, she allowed her next words to flow to him. *"Take absolute care. Hamish's seer ability means he misses little, and being one of the full-blooded fae, his skill is the strongest I've ever seen."*

"I'll take every precaution, my mate." He eased Gordon's boots off and set them against the wall out of the way. *"I've been waiting for you to build a merged link of the mind with me. Those who hold your skill always form such a link with their mate, as well as with a few of their most nearest and trusted."*

"I've only ever opened such a connection with a childhood friend of mine. Fiona held a touch of fae blood, a skill as well, her father being the MacKenzie's second-in-command. We played together often, got into a good deal of trouble when we did as well."

"'Tis incredible to have you speak to me in this way, for me to be able to answer you in return." He lifted Gordon's arm out of the heavy sleeve of metal, slid the protective mail over his head then down his other arm. With a clunk, he set it beside Gordon's boots. *"You've never spoken mind to mind with Coll or Duncan?"*

"Nay." It had seemed too intimate, and even though she currently wished to know how Coll's mission fared and exactly where he was, she would never be able to cross the wide expanse of distance between them. She couldn't even reach her parents, not that she would have done so even if she could. They would have come for her, placed their very lives on the line when they did. *"There are limits to my ability. Since I've been without someone to guide me in the use of it, I lack the skill to do all that I likely could."*

"A little training is all that will take, and I'll ensure you receive that guidance the first moment I can. Tell me more about Fiona." His longing to know everything about her, all that had happened these past twenty years, flared strongly through his mind, just as she longed to know everything about him.

"Somewhere within Fiona's own line the blood of the fae had mingled with hers, although several generations removed. She was the first to have been born with a skill in quite some time, although her empath ability was one Colin MacKenzie

considered weak and feeble. She was grateful though, that he showed no interest in her." She set the paste aside and gathered some clean cloths. "*She wed a warrior of her father's choosing last year and soon after she and Matthew left for Rhue Castle to aid Jeremiah. I missed her dreadfully when she sailed away.*"

"*I've never met Jeremiah in battle, but I'm aware Colin's third-born son is a warrior of immense strength and now holds his own stronghold to the far north of MacKenzie land.*" He loosened the ties of Gordon's chausses and wriggled them down over his braies, his gaze flicking toward Hamish who checked on the bubbling water.

"*Jeremiah is a blackguard just as his father is. Thankfully I've never had to spend a great deal of time with him since he was fostered with the MacLennans.*"

"Does Gordon yet stir?" Hamish added another log.

"No' as yet." And he'd better not either until Ronan had ridden for Ardan and had gotten safely away. She hardly needed Gordon speaking of what had happened before they were ready for him to. Having her chosen one tossed into the dungeons by Gordon wasn't permissible. She'd never allow it.

"What of you, Rand? How did word reach you of Coll's call-to-arms?" Hamish rose and dusted his hands.

"Through word of mouth."

"Hamish, Rand would never harm anyone within this keep. That I can assure you." She motioned for Ronan to remove the bandaging from around Gordon's head and wrist. "He has only ever aided me each time we've met."

"You clearly champion the man, my lady." He dipped his head in reverence to her.

"Aye, I do, for I already know he means us no harm." She swished to the fire, dunked a cloth in the bubbling water and returned to Gordon. Ronan unraveled the bandages and she gently cleansed Gordon's wounds before smearing the plantain paste she'd prepared across his flesh.

"Will he awaken when you stitch his wounds?"

"Nay, and I'll make certain of it." She selected a bottle of belladonna from her medicinal box, dabbed some onto a cloth and draped it over Gordon's nose. The strongly scented sedative would ensure he felt no pain while she stitched his wounds, with the added benefit of keeping him in a deep sleep until she was ready for him to awaken.

She collected her needle and thread, pulled the three-legged stool across from the corner to Gordon's bedside and rolled the sleeve of his brown tunic to his elbow. Carefully, she stitched his wounds closed with nice and neat stitches.

"Since it appears Gordon is at rest and shall be for a while we'll leave for Ardan now." Hamish crossed to Ronan. "Do you still wish to offer your sword arm to our cause?"

"Aye, and I'm more than ready to leave." Ronan caught up his bag from where she'd set it.

"Good." Hamish opened the door and motioned for Ronan to go through first. "Kyla, send word if any issue arises with Gordon, otherwise we'll see you on our return."

"Of course." She snuggled deeper into Ronan's mind. *"Be careful."*

"Stay right with me, for as long as you can. I already crave this connection and have no desire for you to close it off." He strode out the door and clomped downstairs, his booted tread drifting away.

"Dinnae forget what I said afore. Hamish has been instrumental in ensuring all has gone well of late, his knowledge immense. Tell him the truth, allow him to aid you as needed. He would never harm a Matheson." Moving deeper within his mind, she tracked his thoughts and movements, her connection to him strong, far stronger than it had ever been with Fiona.

"I willnae forget, my mate." Through the main door, he walked and as he crossed the inner bailey, he surveyed all, from the training warriors to the position of each and every guard

along the battlements. *"I miss you."*

"*I miss you too.*"

* * * *

The last thing Ronan wished to do was leave Kyla behind, but ensuring her betrothal to Duncan came to a swift end, that the man understood the two of them were mated and he intended on making Kyla his bride, was imperative. He had a great deal to do, would need to act fast. Seeking out her parents as well couldn't be delayed.

Across the inner courtyard, he walked while a good score of warriors trained. Shirtless and sweaty, they fought partnered up, each strike of their blade landing with accurate precision against their opponent's. These men were strong, fully prepared for the war which raged across these lands and throughout the Western Isles. Glad he was none would strike a Matheson, only why had Coll and Duncan made that stipulation with their warriors? Something was up, something he intended to get to the bottom of.

"This way." Hamish led him toward the men's barracks at the edge of the bailey. "I need to collect a few things afore we leave."

"I'm afraid I didnae bring a horse since I had to cross the hills. The land is treacherously steep and heavily forested." A truth. The land was rugged, dangerously so.

"Aye, even our men dinnae take to those hills on horseback. I'll secure you a horse without issue." Hamish walked inside the garrison's front door and Ronan followed, passed dozens of bunked pallets as he strode to the far side.

An unlit fireplace stood at one end of the room and racks of armor gleamed under its flickering light. A young lad of mayhap eight or nine sat on a stool in a brown tunic and breeches. He meticulously cleaned chainmail and weaponry, a large whetstone at his feet and his fingers black with oil.

From within a shelved nook, Hamish snagged a satchel and

stuffed a steel-studded coat inside before he hunkered down next to the lad. "I'm returning to Ardan House and taking with me a possible new recruit. Inform the guardsman on duty for me, and let him know I'll return as soon as possible."

"Aye, sir." The lad scrambled to his feet then stumbled to a stop in front of Ronan and bobbed his head, his mop of unruly dark hair flopping forward over his brow. "My laird, welcome home," he murmured then dashed out the door.

"He thinks you're Coll, as I first did, and as I imagine a number of the men here will when they catch a decent glimpse of you." Hamish tipped his head toward the door. "Come. We'll head through the postern gate to the stables. That way we willnae draw too much unwanted attention to you."

"How many men guard this stronghold?" With a brisk pace, he weaved around the perimeter of the yard and out the postern gate with Hamish.

"Over a hundred, with another hundred at Duncan's keep a little farther along the loch, although our hope is to double our numbers at both strongholds."

"Coll and Duncan prepare well." He followed the stony walkway around the curtain wall toward the stables which sat at the edge of the forest where the trees butted up against the cliffs. A gangly-legged lad in loosely belted pants brushed down a sleek brown war horse, while two armed warriors mounted their steeds then galloped into the bordering forest.

"They must during this time of war." Hamish nodded at the stable lad. "I'm in need of two saddled mounts, and be quick about it."

The lad scurried inside and disappeared within the darkened depths of the stables.

Eyeing him with great curiosity, Hamish leaned against the wide doorway, tapped the heel of one booted foot within the dirt and hummed under his breath. "Interesting."

"You've seen something?"

"That I have." He touched his head. "Glimpses of you within visions, and enough to tell me that Rand isnae your true name."

"My need to speak to Duncan is twofold, yet primarily involves Kyla." The seer definitely held a strong ability.

"'Tis clear to see you hold her trust, unwaveringly so. She is a woman with a tender heart and gentle hand, and there isnae a warrior here who wouldnae lay down his life for hers. I also 'see' that you'd be the first one standing in line to do so."

"Tell him I'm in your mind, have seen and heard all he's said."

"You are persistent, my mate."

"And I always shall be. Give Hamish your trust. **He willnae have you tossed into the dungeons.**"

With a deep breath, he nodded at Hamish. "What if I told you Kyla speaks to me now? Has formed a merged link of the mind?"

"Then that would mean she's told you of her fae blood, and if that's the case then it appears you've garnered far more than just her trust."

"Aye, that is true." A seagull soared overhead, cackled then dove into the tumbling waters of the loch before heaving back up out of the white-capped surf with a fish flapping from its beak.

"I—" Hamish's gaze clouded over. He squeezed his eyes shut then moments later opened them again. "Aye, there is no doubt in my mind now of your identity. You're Ronan Matheson, Niall's son, and since your father has recently completed the bond with my sister, that makes you and I very close kin. This is beyond interesting." He pushed off the doorway, paced back and forth. "I see more. You long to visit your father, to ensure all is truly well with him even though your sister has made contact with him through her fae skill."

"My father has chosen to remain with Muirin instead of returning to the village and that I cannae fault him for. They are soul bound."

"Two horses saddled, sir." The lad led two black destriers out, handed the reins of one to Hamish and the other to him.

As Hamish strapped his bag onto his horse, he thanked the lad then bounded into his saddle and eyed Ronan. "We must travel swiftly since Duncan will wish to speak to you, just as you wish to speak to him. Although I shall pave the way in making your coming meeting easier. What your father has learnt of recently, so too will you."

"Whatever aid you can offer me will be greatly appreciated." He fastened his satchel to his horse's saddle, checked the cinch and mounted. Reins slapped against his beast's neck, he galloped out of the yard right alongside Hamish. They rode up the cliff side trail, the waves crashing in on his left and the forest rising high on his right. Leaving Kyla behind hurt, each stride his horse took making his gut gnaw in the most vicious way. 'Twas pure agony when his emotions battled so strongly against each other. All he wanted to do right now was turn his mount back around and return to her. *"How do you fare?"*

"Better now Hamish is aware of who you are." Softly spoken words that curled around his senses.

"Tell me exactly what Kyla means to you." Lying low in his saddle, Hamish jumped over trailing tree roots, the higher branches skimming his head.

"She's the woman I've been searching for my entire life, the woman I intend to wed, or at least I shall once I've spoken to Duncan and explained to him the intricacies of the mated bond, that I'll never allow him to speak vows with her. She is my chosen one." He rode hard as the skies darkened overhead.

"And now I have my answer for why she championed you so strongly." Approval flickered in Hamish's eyes. "In all honesty, I never did see her marrying Duncan even though word of their betrothal made its way to me this morn."

"Speaking of her betrothal. Kyla fears Colin MacKenzie's wrath and his threat to harm her parents should she ever go against his demand to wed one of his sons. I intend to make certain her parents learn of what's occurred, that they take every precaution to guard and protect themselves against any possible attack, action I'll need to take as soon as I've spoken to Duncan." He tucked himself lower and tighter against his horse's neck as they weaved up the winding trail. Stones scattered along the gravelly track, flew over the cliff's verge and rapped down the rock face before disappearing into the churning, watery depths below.

"I'll aid you as you need." Knees tight to his horse's flanks, Hamish nudged his mount on. "It truly is time for the fae to live. Past time. I'm also well aware Duncan wants you fighting on our side, had even intended on offering you a lucrative incentive to sway you, that's afore our fae princess arrived and rescued you from Carron's dungeons. Cherub has no knowledge of exactly why Muirin and I are here, but she soon will. All happens as it should, in its own time and even we fae cannae fight against that."

"You said you would pave the way in making my coming meeting with Duncan easier. What is it my father has learnt of recently, that so too will I?"

"Aye, I shall speak of that now. Prepare yourself." Hamish breathed deep, as if he too prepared himself. "Coll and Duncan hold fae blood."

"Pardon?"

"'Tis past time you were made aware, just as your father has been."

"Tell me all." Shock rippled through him.

"Your father had a younger sister by the name of Beth. Are you aware of her, of how she came to pass away?"

"Aye. She died the year I was born. My father spoke of her often during my childhood, his love for her strong. She held the skill of death-warning and during a time of peace between clan Matheson and clan MacKenzie, she handfasted with a MacKenzie warrior. She conceived and after a difficult labor gave birth to twins, both of whom passed away. My father's sister perished along with them. A tragedy for certain."

"'Twas no' one of the MacKenzie's warriors whom Beth handfasted with, but Colin MacKenzie himself, and the two babes she carried survived, didnae perish as she did."

Surely not. His father had never heard that truth. "Are you certain?"

"Beyond certain. Colin MacKenzie kept Beth locked within her chamber, although a few days afore Beth's death she saw a vision through her skill. Beth saw her own demise and she pleaded with Colin to send a message to Grace, her childhood friend who held the same skill as her."

"Grace? As in Kyla's mother?" More shock.

"Aye, and after Grace arrived at Beth's bedside, she gave Beth her word she'd watch over her newborn babes. Grace kept her promise, even remained at the MacKenzie's stronghold for the first three years of Coll and Duncan's lives, until the day when war once again broke out between the clans and she was forced to return to her village or else become a pawn in the war."

Hell, Coll and Duncan were Beth's sons, which meant they were his cousins. Along with shock, anger and frustration coursed fiercely through him. Damn the MacKenzie. Now he understood why Coll and Duncan had never raised a hand in battle against a Matheson. They couldn't slay one of their own fae kind any more than he could. "I wish I'd known sooner. Why did Grace keep the knowledge of their true parentage to herself? She has never spoken a word in all these years, could so easily have done so."

"Grace had no choice, just as Coll and Duncan never have. Kyla either. Coll and Duncan only learnt the truth about their birth at the age of eight when Grace had a vision of them and returned to the MacKenzie's keep to warn the boys, just as Beth had asked her to do should such a thing occur."

"Mama took me with her that night. 'Twas only a few days afore the MacKenzie returned to the village and abducted me." Solemn words, heavy and filled with such pain and heartache. *"At the time Mama needed to ensure the boys understood exactly what must be done to safeguard their future. She told them to never raise a hand against a Matheson, for to do so would be to harm their own kind. Only a handful of people have ever known the truth about their fae heritage, and you now are amongst that small number."*

"They are my aunt's sons, close kin through and through." To Hamish, he gritted out, "Do Coll and Duncan hold a fae skill?"

"Aye, the battle skill, just as you and your father do."

"Why did the MacKenzie keep this all a secret?"

"If he'd allowed the truth to be known, then he'd have lost not only the lucrative lands he came by with his marriage to Cait MacLennan, but also would have incurred the wrath of the MacLennan chief himself. They are close allies and that bond would've been severed once he'd learnt the truth of the MacKenzie's deceit."

"I'm sorry you've had to keep this secret as well, Kyla. That cannae have been easy."

"Coll and Duncan might be the Chief of MacKenzie's sons, but they are naught like him and never have been. Their hearts are loyal to their fae kind."

"There is more," Hamish added. "Grace has never spoken the truth for fear of Colin's reprisal. He threatened her, said should she ever disclose the truth then he'd attack her village and slaughter one and all. Through her death-warning skill, she saw that he would do so, and through my seer ability, so have I."

"My mama continues to remain quiet because that threat remains in place. She would have spoken up otherwise."

"I agree. She's a nurturer and protector, would never have allowed the death of another to occur at her hand." Another new fierce level of respect and admiration for his mate roared through him, for Grace too. These two women had done what was best for their clan for the past two decades, and regardless of the pain it had caused them both, they'd accepted their fate. He rode on in silence, Hamish right at his side, the skies darkening further as night loomed, his own heart heaving at the loss they'd all suffered because of one man. Colin MacKenzie. In time, he'd make certain the man paid for all he'd done. He'd ensure it.

Chapter 4

Sitting in the corner blue padded chair next to the crackling fire with its bubbling pot of water, Kyla opened her eyes, her mind still deeply entrenched within Ronan's. *"I truly wish I could be there when you speak to Duncan."*

"You will be, through our connection. It still holds, even across the miles I've now ridden." His deep and husky words shimmered through her mind. *"Because of your skill, we'll never be far apart."*

"Aye, you're right. I love my skill, more so now than ever afore." Beyond the window, an owl hooted as the dark of the night rolled in. This morning she'd begun the day so lost and alone out on the cliffs, and now she'd not only been reunited with her chosen one, but her entire future had changed, or at least she would hold the firm hope that it had.

She pushed up and plucked another log from the wood pile next to the hearth and tossed it on the fire. The flames sizzled and spread a golden-red glow throughout the chamber. She closed the shutters over the window and crossed to Gordon.

His breath continued to move with a steady flow in and out, no further blood loss dampening his bandages, although his forehead was bruised black and blue, the lump protruding high.

He'd sleep without issue for what remained of the night, the belladonna ensuring that, and in the morn when he awoke, she'd examine him once more.

Assured all was well, she closed the door behind her and tramped upstairs to her room on the third floor. A maid had built a roaring fire for her, as well as closed the thick red drapes over her window overlooking the inner courtyard. She passed the crackling blaze of peat and wood, foraged for her nightgown in the trunk at the end of her four-poster bed then stepped behind her silk dressing screen hand-painted with pink and purple heather. Front stays unlaced and her gown's bodice scrunched in her hands, she snuggled deeper within Ronan's mind.

"Kyla, wait." His croaky voice stayed her hands.

"Is something wrong?"

"As you can see through my eyes, so too I can see through yours."

"I'm well aware." With a mischievous giggle, she dropped her gown. The rich midnight-blue fabric slithered to the polished floorboards and she stepped out of the pool of velvet, scooped it up and tossed it over top of the screen. In just her shift, she gripped the hem. *"Would you like for me to continue? I wish to ready myself for bed."*

"Aye, nay, aye. I mean halt."

"I dinnae wish for there to be any more secrets between us."

"Thank heavens you've never created this link with another man." A fierce growl. *"Leave your shift on. You can sleep in that."*

"Are you certain?" She dropped the hem, palmed the undersides of her breasts through the cotton and scooped them higher, rubbed her thumbs over her nipples and gasped at the delicious tingles that raced across her skin. Never had she touched herself in such a brazen way before and 'twas most, ah, interesting.

"Do you want me to fall off my horse? I have no' done that since I was a lad."

"Nay, I dinnae wish to have to tend any more injuries this night." She sashayed out from behind the screen. *"What a shame you're so far away."*

"More than a shame."

She nabbed her brush from her side table and combed her hair, washed her teeth with a mint and salt paste, splashed her face with cool water from the basin then dived into bed and snuggled between the crisp white sheets, her red and gold patterned bedcover tucked under her chin. 'Twas a quilt she'd made herself. As a child Mama had taught her how to sew squares of beautifully colored fabric together to create a pattern and she'd done so with this red and gold silk, the design reflecting a rainbow of the two striking hues. Mama's favorite colors and Papa's too. Each night when she fell asleep, 'twas with thoughts of her parents close to her heart.

Eyes closed, she tracked Ronan's movements, followed him as he galloped through the dark and down the winding cliff top trail until he came out next to the secluded bay near Duncan's stronghold. The fortified walls of Ardan House rose out of the dark and the guardsman standing on duty at the gatehouse bellowed the warning of their arrival.

Both men slowed their horses as they passed the sea-gate where a powerful war galley bobbed from its mooring at the end of the landing. Duncan's vessel. He adored the sea, sailing along Scotland's western coastline and in and about the isles. Through the main gate, Ronan and Hamish rode under the high arch, their horses heaving misty air as they brought them to a stop within the inner courtyard.

Torches mounted on the curtain wall spread their flickering glow across the stony ground and up toward the battlements where Duncan's warriors patrolled in battle attire, their weapons holstered at their sides and stance strong. 'Twas a heavily fortified keep, even more so than Carron Castle.

Hamish jumped from his horse and landed with a clomp on the gravel, handed his reins to a stable lad who rushed forward to take them then marched across the yard to the front door and halted on the step underneath the eaves. He eyed Ronan who still sat atop his horse surveying the bailey and all within it. "Are you coming?"

"Aye, I'm coming." He dismounted, handed his reins to the lad who waited and followed Hamish inside. *"Stay with me."*

"Always." This coming meeting was one she'd never miss out on. She remained embedded deeply within Ronan's mind as he prepared himself for the conversation to come, for this night he'd not only speak to Duncan, but also be close once again to his father after being parted for nigh on a month. *"I'm sorry you were kept separated from your father during your imprisonment. If there had been any other way, Duncan would have taken it, but Hamish had seen that both yours and your father's capture was needed in order for Muirin to have the chance to convince Niall of their mated bond. Your father wouldnae have come willingly to her otherwise, no' while she remained on MacKenzie land and our clans so fiercely at war. Neither could we have told you the truth until the time was right. Our fae princess might have intervened and changed things."*

* * * *

"I've accepted all that happened, have no issue since my capture brought me to you." With one hand firm on the hilt of his side belted sword, he strode into the great hall with its vaulted ceiling and high wooden beamed rafters. Large tapestries of the countryside covered the walls, and a dozen or more trestle tables had been pushed to one side with a good fifty sleeping pallets laid down before the roaring fire. Warriors had already bedded down for the night, men wearing both the MacKenzie plaid as he did, and the MacRae tartan. *"Why are there so many warriors from clan MacRae here?"*

"One of the MacRae chief's sons now possesses a large parcel of land to the south of us and has forged an alliance with Coll and Duncan. The younger MacRae has wed a lass who holds a touch of fae blood and wishes only to ensure her protection and that of their son. His eldest is only four and holds the 'power of thought.' He can levitate, move objects and people, and all with only a thought from his mind alone." Kyla sent a wave of warmth and love down their link, wrapped him fully in it. *"Muirin aids the young lad in his training and Coll and Duncan have moved swiftly to ensure she can without issue. Certainly should Colin ever get his hands on the lad, I shudder to think what would become of him."*

"At the village, we have two who hold the same skill. They could aid the lad in his training as well if required." He'd make the offer to whomever he must another time. For now, he followed Hamish around the perimeter of the hall and into a side antechamber holding a large table and chairs.

Hamish crossed to the other side of the room and knocked on a partially opened door. "'Tis Hamish."

"Come in."

That voice Ronan would never mistake, not when it belonged to his most beloved parent. Grinning, he jogged past Hamish and rushed inside. Behind a chunky oak desk in the chief's solar, Father sat, his blond hair holding a streak of silver on one side. "Father."

"Ronan?" With his sword sheathed at his side, Father shoved to his feet in gray pants and a thick fur vest. Face awash with astonishment, he swept around the desk. "I realize 'tis been a month since I last saw you, but you've changed a great deal in that time." Father grasped his arms. "What is with those lips of yours? Did a bee sting you?"

"Several bees, and so much has happened since our joint capture." He hauled Father into his arms and held him close, such relief at seeing him flowing through him. "Are you well?"

"Very, and how on earth are you here with Hamish?" Shaking his head, Father stared at him with such bewilderment. Not surprising. The same emotion still consumed him with all he'd learnt this day.

"I needed to sneak back into Carron Castle and claim my chosen one, and preferably without alerting the guards as to whom I was. Kyla holds fae blood and the mind-walker skill, is Grace and Isaiah's lost daughter, Christina."

"Kyla has accepted you and your bond?"

"She will, as soon as I clear up a matter of who she is currently betrothed to."

"What betrothal do you speak of?"

"Duncan has no' told you?"

"I havenae seen Duncan since he rode in."

"I heard visitors have arrived." With a great plaid belted at his waist and looped over one shoulder, a claymore glinting at his side, Duncan strode in and cast his gaze from Hamish to Father then him. "Coll?" A deep frown. "What are you doing back?"

"This isnae Coll." Father clapped Ronan on the shoulder. "Duncan, meet Ronan, my son."

"Hell, your resemblance to my brother is so strong, yet you look naught as you did the last time we met." Duncan stepped closer. "Your hair is dark, your beard gone and that mouth..."

"Aye, my mouth is fuller." He rubbed his plump lips. "I had need to disguise my appearance to begin with in order to get into Carron, had no idea though that in doing so I'd end up looking exactly like Coll, my cousin."

"You're aware Coll and I are your cousins?"

"Hamish explained the details surrounding your birth, 'saw' that he could speak to me of it, and glad I am that he did." No matter Duncan had captured him and Father, separated them afterward and had him contained within Carron's cells while he'd brought Father here, he'd still done so in order to give

Muirin the chance to meet his parent and accept their bond. That he couldn't fault Duncan for. "I only wish I'd known of your fae blood sooner. It would have made all the difference."

"Coll and I take great care with whom we tell." Duncan glanced at Hamish. "What else might you have seen?"

"Ronan's loyalty belongs to Kyla, his father and his closest kin, which now includes you and Coll." Hamish leaned one hip against the wall, his black leather vest pulled tight across his shoulders. "I saw all would be well should I tell him the truth, and he needed to learn of it, just as Niall has."

"Then it appears I owe you an apology, Ronan." Duncan extended his hand to him. "My guardsmen mistreated you during your imprisonment, and after I'd given them explicit instructions no' to. Their orders were to keep you contained within the cells due to your battle skill, but never to lay a hand upon you as they did. They were punished for their transgression then sent away."

"Apology accepted." He shook Duncan's hand.

"That easily, that quickly?"

"I've no need to hold a grudge, and in all honesty, I intend to ask a request of you, one you're no' permitted to turn down. I've returned for Kyla. Your foster sister holds the other half of my soul, has formed a merged link of the mind with me and right now sees all I see and hears all I hear. She is the one my soul hungers for, the only woman I'll ever desire. I ask that you break your betrothal with her, immediately."

"Coll and I brought Kyla here for a reprieve from our father." Duncan grasped his shoulder. "I've no wish to lose her. I love her, have since the day she came to live at my father's keep. Coll and I have ensured her protection and she'll always be ours to love and protect. Provided you can accept Coll and I in her life, that you treat her with all the respect she deserves, then I'll gladly step aside."

"I will guard her life with mine, and certainly never allow Colin MacKenzie near her again."

"As I would guard your life with mine too, my stubborn mate." Sweetly sensual words, ones he clasped ahold of and kept close to his heart.

"Will you marry me, Kyla?"

"You're mine, Ronan Matheson, always mine. Give Duncan my thanks, and tell him I love him too, but I surely am relieved I'll never have to suffer through another one of his slobbery kisses."

"You two have kissed?" He fisted his hands.

"Once, only once, and 'twas a terrible kiss." She wriggled about in her bed.

"Then answer my question. Will you marry me?"

"Ask me in person and I shall give you my answer, one which will require an abundance of kisses from you."

"I intend to do far more than just kiss you the next time I get my hands on you." To Duncan, he muttered, "You have Kyla's thanks, as well as mine. She also says she loves you."

"Good evening, all." A woman dressed in an exquisite silver gown with long draping sleeves edged in gold lace swished into the solar, a torque necklace of fine gold encircling her neck. Her iridescent eyes shimmered as she halted a breath away from Father and tucked her hand through the curve of his arm. "Would you like to introduce me to the man who looks exceedingly like Coll, but of course isnae?"

"Muirin, meet my son, Ronan. Kyla and Ronan are mated, and Duncan has graciously retracted his betrothal with her."

"Oh my. I've been gone for only a few minutes and have missed so much." Muirin's iridescent eyes reflected such an array of colors, both breathtakingly fearsome to behold yet also undeniably beautiful. With her high cheeks, flawless skin, and rich red locks twisted high upon her head, the odd strand clinging to the long column of her neck, she was of clear fae blood, her face untouched by age yet her very presence speaking of the centuries of knowledge she must hold. She crossed to

Ronan. "'Tis good to meet you."

"As it is to meet you."

"Your arrival here gives me the chance to apologize for my part in your capture and imprisonment. I'd been searching for your father for the longest time and when two are soul bound, neither can ignore the bond, particularly me. I've lived a long time and never thought I'd ever find my chosen one. All was made so much more difficult in that I resided here on his enemy's soil."

"We do what we must to find our chosen one, to draw them to our side. I no longer hold any hard feelings toward you." He would gladly accept his father's mate, no matter she'd first stolen Father away from him and Annella. She'd done so for the right reasons. Soul bound mates would do anything to ensure they never lost the one who held the other half of their soul and Muirin had acted as he would have done should their circumstances have been reversed. Nothing and no one would ever keep him from Kyla.

"Thank you." Muirin cleared her throat, a tear in her eye. "I wish only to protect those of fae blood who walk this Earth." She lifted one sleeve and tapped a mark branded on her upper arm, that of the ancient Celtic woven circle, one depicting *infinity*, the symbol of their fae kind. "There is naught I wouldnae do for my own kind, no matter where they reside, either here on Earth or beyond the veil."

Sincerity laced her words and he dipped his head in acknowledgement. 'Twas time for a new beginning, for all of them. He'd been gifted with a mate, two cousins, and now a new mother when he'd been bereft of one for so very long.

"I've seen how deep your love for your fae kind is this past month." Father squeezed Muirin's hand. "Have discovered my ice queen has thawed and become someone I admire. 'Tis time for the fae to live, including all of us."

"Here, here," Duncan cheered. "A saying both Coll and I

have embraced since the day Grace said those very words to us after her vision. Never will we forget them."

"Speaking of visions." Hamish grunted, his brown eyes clouding over. He grabbed the back of the closest chair and leaned against it. "'Tis another, and a rather strong one at that."

"What do you see?" Muirin grasped Hamish's arm and rubbed his back. "Speak."

"I see Jeremiah and Colin MacKenzie." He groaned, knuckles whitening around the wood. "Jeremiah confronts his father. Oh hell. Jeremiah's livid, has just learnt the truth about Kyla's fae blood. Colin said 'twas time." He shoved his eyes open, his gaze clearing as it landed on Ronan. "Jeremiah sails now for Carron Castle. He wants what he's been denied, the chance to make Kyla his bride. We need to leave, now."

"I'll allow no one to take Kyla from me, never again." Ronan raced for the door, Duncan and Hamish one step behind him. She was his, and he'd ensure it.

* * * *

Bolting upright in bed, Kyla squinted through the dark toward the window as the head guardsman's shout resounded. She shoved the covers back and hopped across the cold polished planks and gripped the windowsill. The skies had lightened a touch, dawn so very close. She hadn't meant to fall asleep after hearing of Hamish's vision, not while Ronan rode so hard to return to her, but sheer exhaustion had taken ahold and she'd slipped under.

"Raise the portcullis!" The clunky rattle of the chains reverberated across the yard.

Horses' hooves pounded then three riders galloped under the arch and hauled their mounts to a stop. The warrior at the party's head bounded from his destrier in thick black boots, his plaid belted around his waist and claymore swaying at his side. Ronan. His short black hair blazed blue on the ends, was messed by the wind and when he glanced upward and found her at her window, his piercing golden gaze narrowed in on her and stated one thing loud and clear. He was coming, and wouldn't be halted.

He stormed through the main doors while Duncan bellowed orders to his guardsmen on the battlements to secure the keep. The portcullis cranked down, the main gate swiftly barred, the postern gate too. The yard swarmed with men.

Wringing her hands, she paced her chamber, fussed with her hair, her fingers getting stuck within the usual frizzy mess she made of it when she slept at night.

A knock rattled the door and Ronan stepped inside, shut the door behind him and slid the bolt home. He scrutinized her from head to foot. "You. Fell. Asleep."

"I didnae mean to."

"I couldnae stand the loss of our connection." He dropped his satchel next to the bed, unfastened his sword belt and propped his weapon against the headboard then unlaced his boots and toed them off. Leather jerkin unbuttoned and removed, he hauled his black tunic over his head, tossed his clothing on the upholstered red and gold brocade wingchair and dressed only in his kilt, halted in front of her.

"You are making yourself quite at home." She touched one finger to his chest, swirled down over his golden skin then traced along the waistband of his tartan.

"From this moment forth, your bedchamber is my bedchamber." He dipped his head, touched his forehead to hers. "I also intend on making you my wife, in every single way. Would you do me the great honor of marrying me, Kyla?"

"Aye, I would love to be your wife." Excitement buzzed through her and she shuffled closer, touched the tips of her toes to his toes.

"Then I wish for you to wear my ring." He removed a glittering ring from his sporran and taking her hand in his, set it on her palm.

"Oh my." A large diamond with two beautiful sapphires either side sparkled bright atop a shiny band of gold. "'Tis so beautiful. Where did you get this from?"

"During the weeks I spent recovering at Ivanson in the twenty-first century, I had the chance to visit a village where I came across what they call a jewelry store. Within that store sat an array of glass-enclosed cases with a dazzling number of rings and other beautiful trinkets and charms. When I saw this ring with its two sapphires, the same exquisite color of your blue eyes, I couldnae pass it by. I offered the owner of the store one of my daggers for the ring and he graciously accepted, said he'd never seen the likes of such a well-kept piece of ancient weaponry." He brought her fingers to his lips and kissed each one. "I wish to bind myself to you for the rest of my days. Speak handfast vows with me and I promise once a priest can be procured, we'll be wed proper."

"Handfast vows can too easily be broken. Jeremiah is on his way. He is devious, just as his father is, will demand his right to a betrothal. Afore Coll and Duncan brought me here, I gave Colin MacKenzie my word I'd wed one of his sons. I had no other choice, no' if I wished to travel so far from him."

"Duncan will never allow Jeremiah near you, and neither shall I. Should we consummate our handfast vows then there'll be far less of a chance Jeremiah can make any demands on you that will hold. Think only of keeping your word to me, of the oath which you gave me by the pool." He pulled out a strip of Matheson plaid from his sporran, clasped his right hand with her right and wound the tartan of her true clan around both their wrists, the ring held firm between their clasped palms.

Tears misted her gaze. This tartan was one she hadn't touched in over twenty years and now it would bind them together in matrimony. His gesture spoke to her very heart, made those tears fall free and slide down her cheeks.

"Nay, dinnae cry." He scooped her up, sat on the end of the

bed and cradled her on his lap. "Please, no tears."

"These tears are good tears, and this feels like a dream to be here with you right now." Her heart lifted, such joy encompassing her. "I want to keep my word to you."

"I need you." The look in his eyes burned hungry and hot. "I want your hands all over me, for you to touch me as you did beside the pool, but this time when we both reach that peak together, I want my cock buried deep inside you."

Warmth flushed her cheeks, his words heating her from within. She wanted that too, more than wanted it. "You say the naughtiest things." Grinning and emboldened, she pushed him onto his back and straddled his thighs. "Since the moment you escaped Duncan's dungeons, I feared your return, yet also secretly desired it. I wanted to be claimed by you, but I also had no desire to take you from your own fae kind and set you squarely within the ranks of your enemy." She wriggled one finger between their clasped palms, slid the ring free and eased it onto her finger. "I want to speak handfast vows with you, then you must ride out and return with a priest, with all haste."

"Of course. I'll begin." He cleared his throat, his gaze holding her captive. "I, Ronan Niall Matheson, of the House of Clan Matheson, pledge my troth to Kyla, of Carron Castle. With this handfast, I take her as my wife for the next year and a day, and as my chosen one for all time." He tightened his grip on her hand. "'Tis your turn."

"Aye, my turn." She breathed deep, her fingers twined firmly with his. "I, Kyla, of Carron Castle, pledge my troth to Ronan Niall Matheson, of the House of Clan Matheson. With this handfast, I take him as my husband for the next year and a day, and as my chosen one for all time." She touched the plaid bound around their wrists, her heart lifting even farther. "I will be Kyla Matheson from this day forth, once again taking my true clan's name."

"Aye, as you should have from the very beginning." He

plucked the tartan free, captured her face in his hands and gently stroked his fingers back and forth over her cheeks. "Any other requests other than that I ride out for a priest with all haste?"

"You must speak to my parents immediately and let them know of the danger they're now in." She covered his hands with hers, snuggled her cheeks deeper into his palms.

"I'll ensure they're made aware of the danger, to always be on the lookout. I adore your parents and have since the very beginning, would never wish any harm to fall upon them." He stroked his thumbs over her lower lip. "Following your disappearance, I visited them often. Doing so brought me closer to you, even though we had no knowledge of where you were. All your mama knew was that she'd never seen a vision of death-warning hovering over you. Such an inquisitive child you were, always wandering here and there and your papa searched far and wide for you, listened out for any who might have heard of a lost child. Never did he hear a word or even receive a demand for coin. They were at such a loss for what had truly happened."

"They never considered the MacKenzie had taken me?"

"Unfortunately we have many enemies, clans who both covet and fear our fae blood. They wish to have what we have, as well as destroy it too. The MacKenzie is only one of amongst many, and he's never gone so far as to steal one of our children away. His preference is for warring and that alone."

"Are they well? My parents?" She adored that he'd been so near them.

"You've never tried to even touch their minds to see, just once?" Such compassion shone in his gaze.

"Nay, to begin with I was too young and couldnae cross the distance, my skill too weak, then as the years passed, I feared the pain and heartache if I did since there was naught I could do to return to them. I certainly cannae reach them from here. The distance is too great." Such love for her parents filled her heart. "I'll never forget Mama's smile and her big blue eyes, as well as

Papa's immense love for her, the way he always stole a kiss from Mama afore he walked out of the house. I've kept them in my heart all these years, just as I know they've kept me in theirs."

"They love you, will understand why you've remained quiet all this time. You sought only to ensure their protection, a most admirable trait." He palmed the back of her head, drew her closer, his gaze burning a smoldering golden hue. "As I shall now ensure their protection and yours. Afore I ride out, we need to consummate our vows. Are you ready?"

"More than ready."

Chapter 5

All Ronan had ever desired since the moment he'd walked into Kyla's chamber and found her anxiously awaiting him, was to speak vows with her then make ravenous love until they'd exhausted each other. "I want to remove your shift. Is that permissible?" He traced over the beaded tips of her nipples poking through the thin white fabric, the glow from the fire behind her outlining every inch of her womanly curves.

"Very, provided you also remove your kilt." Sitting over top of him, she wriggled and her saucy move made his already hard cock harden further.

"Ladies first." He needed to learn her body, every delectable plane and heavenly contour before she ever touched him. "Arms up."

"As you wish." She raised her hands and her full breasts rose.

He'd been waiting an entire lifetime for this moment, to have his chosen one as his wife and he gripped her hem, lifted it over her spread legs and exposed her womanhood. His throat went dry. Luscious golden curls sat at her juncture and he touched one finger to her mound as he lifted his gaze back to hers. "You're about to be mine."

"I've always been yours." She swayed and sighed. "Touch me, all of me."

"I dinnae intend to leave one inch of you untouched, either by my hands or my tongue. Consider that fair warning." His chosen one was all he'd ever hoped for in a mate. She was feisty and determined, prepared to do all she could for her closest kin. Aye, she was his match in every way and now he had her behind a locked door and all to himself, he intended to love her exactly as he desired. No more waiting. He peeled her shift higher, over her flat belly until the undersides of her bountiful breasts became exposed. He groaned as a fiery burn blazed at the base of his spine.

"You are taking far too long in undressing me." She snuck the hem from his fingers, swept her shift over her head and tossed it aside.

"Hell, you're so beautiful." He could barely breathe at the sight of her body fully uncovered for him. Her decadently creamy skin beckoned and he trailed his fingers down between the valley of her breasts until she arched and thrust her breasts out farther. Accepting all she offered, he cupped the exquisite fullness, weighed both mounds in his hands then eased them together and swiped his thumbs over the beaded tips. Elbows shoved underneath him, he lifted up a little and licked one tempting nipple.

"More," she whimpered, her eyelids fluttering closed.

"Aye, more." He flipped her onto her back and she squealed at his fast move. "Stay still, my bride, because I intend to consume you."

"Oh goodness." Her breathing came harder, the desire in her blue eyes blazing bright.

"I promise I'll take the utmost care." Everything about her called to him, from her breasts tipped with rosy nipples all puckered and straining toward him, to the long curve of her creamy flesh on display and the delicate lines of her face. In this moment, she'd given him her complete trust and he never intended on breaking it, not now, not ever.

On his knees between her legs, he swept his hands down her body, over her flat belly and across her hips which would cradle his to sheer perfection when they joined together. Such sweetly curved thighs, beguiling calves and dainty toes. His bride's body was one to worship and adore. He leaned in, rubbed his cheek over the satiny soft skin of her midriff, her alluring fragrance, all woman with a touch of vanilla, swirling about him. He wriggled lower, nuzzled the thatch of golden curls covering her mound then licked along each indented line of her groin.

"Ronan?" Eyes closed, she fisted the bedcovers either side of her and arched her back.

"Aye." He slid his fingers over her lower folds. "Do you wish for this kind of touch?"

"Immensely."

"You're so lush and exquisitely pink right here." He pushed one finger deep inside her channel, lifted his head and seized her mouth with his. He kissed her while down below, he fondled her passage and stroked over her nub.

"Dinnae cease touching me so." She nipped his lower lip. "I want all that you want, the pleasure, the joining, all of you inside of me."

"You are going to make the perfect wife." Kissing her, he delved into the sweetly warm recesses of her mouth, her entire body bared for him alone and every inch of her his to taste and treasure. With his finger, he continued to massage her inner channel as he built her pleasure, then added a second finger and pushed even deeper. He needed to stretch her wonderfully tight passage and as gently as he could if he intended on keeping any pain from their joining to a minimum.

His cock ached with an incessant pounding, his balls drawing tighter and his essence leaking from the head. If only he could alleviate some of this pressure building inside him as well.

He rolled his hips against hers, but to no avail. That action only tightened his cock to the point of pain and he groaned.

"Let me touch you, as I did at the pool." She gripped the belt holding his kilt in place and unbuckled it, pushed the heavy folds of tartan aside and licked her lips as his erection poked into her belly. Blue eyes twinkling, she touched her finger to the head of his shaft, swirled along the slit and rubbed the drops of pre-come oozing free. "Can I tell you a secret?"

"Always."

"Beside the pool, as we kissed and touched each other, when you came and your essence shot from you, I lay on my back afterward with your seed glistening on my fingertips and wished that you'd come inside me instead. In that moment, I wanted my choices taken from me, so that I no longer had to consider anyone else except you. Now I'm about to get my wish, to join with you now as I'd fervently wished to then." Carefully, she cupped his balls with one hand and wrapped her fingers around his shaft with the other. "I am yours, Ronan, as you are mine. None can ignore this bond, no' even I."

"Aye, as it shall always be." He kissed her, suckled her tongue between his lips and she moaned into his mouth, tightened her grip on his cock, her fingers so wickedly firm he almost shot his load right then and there. Hell, her exquisite touch would be his undoing and since he intended for her to find her pleasure first, he needed to take firm action. He shuffled back, lost her exquisite hold on his cock as he did, but got her entire body as a platter to feast on. Hands underneath her bottom, he caressed her firm lower cheeks, his mouth watering for all she offered. "I want to touch you, everywhere."

"I want to touch you too."

"Later, much later." He grinned at the sight of her inner flesh, all his for the taking. Nose pressed to the curls covering her entrance, he breathed deep and got lost in the heady sensations washing over him. He licked along her inner thighs, first one side and then the other until he reached her folds where her womanhood beckoned him. He stroked along her slit. So wet. So gloriously wet.

"Wait." She tangled her fingers in his hair and held onto him, as if her very life depended on it. His certainly did.

"No more waiting." Licking across her flesh, he moved his mouth over her sensitive nub and sucked, hard. He gorged himself on her, the only woman who would ever be his.

"Ronan." Her bottom went tight under his palms. "I cannae hold on if you keep touching me like this.

"Then let go. Show me your pleasure, that it has come at my hands alone." He lunged in and consumed her, drawing her pleasure to a steep pinnacle and as she cried out and shuddered in his arms, he thrust two fingers deep inside her inner channel and groaned as she pulsed around his fingers and sucked them in with such a greedy pull. "I need to be inside you."

"Mmm, aye, please," she murmured as she slumped back on the bed, her eyes closed and an expression of pure bliss crossing her face, one he never wished to see disappear.

With his achingly hard shaft in his hand and a powerful surge of desire slamming through him, he rubbed the head of his cock over her drenched folds, his desperation to join with her at its most intense. He'd waited forever for this moment, his need feverish and all-consuming.

* * * *

Kyla's core pulsed with the pleasure Ronan had given her and when she opened her eyes, she almost lost her breath at the deep whirlpool of need churning within his gaze. The rising sun beamed through her window and splayed over his broad shoulders and muscled chest covered in a sprinkling of fine golden hair. She drew in one very necessary breath, the width and breadth of him so impressive. Her chosen one held the battle skill, trained daily with the sword and never was that more obvious as he loomed over her, all big and powerful.

She swished along the line of golden hair narrowing down between the defined ridges of his abs, trailed lower as the hair thickened into lush curls around his erect cock. His shaft rose thick and strong from within the nest of pale hair, the plump head pulsing a rich and ripe color, his hand fisted tight around himself.

"Since the moment you came to me in the dungeons"—he pressed the head of his cock to her entrance—"I envisioned this day, of us joining fully together as one. This is all I've ever craved, to be with you in every single way."

"Then make it so." She hooked her legs around the backs of his legs and he groaned and slid against her. He was all hers and she couldn't halt her need. She allowed her mind-walker skill to rise, tunneled deeper inside his mind and gasped at the barrage of powerful and raw emotions within, his need for her one that burned all the way to his very soul. Along their connection, one she tightened between them, she whispered, *"I want this, for you to be inside me, so none can dispute you're my husband, in every way."*

"Before we consummate our vows, I need to ask something of you." He kissed her, his chest pressed against her breasts, his cock poised at her entrance where with one push, he'd be buried deep within. *"The moment I breach your barrier, I want you to fuse this link you've created with me within my mind, permanently and fully. It can be done and once it has been, I too will be able to reach you by opening our fused connection. That is the way of your skill between soul bound mates, the connection one that grows into a complete fullness unlike any other."*

"I wasnae aware such a fusing was possible." If it was, she wanted that link. *"You can truly reach me once I do as you say?"*

"Aye, and you would have known of it had you been taught about your ability by our elders. You have missed a great deal of training, but no more. I'll ensure your instruction begins the first moment I can."

"Then make us one and I shall do exactly as you've asked and fuse the link."

"Aye, no more shall we wait." He reached between them, fondled her nub, his intimate touch exactly what she needed and as she rocked underneath him, he thrust his cock inside, tore through her barrier below and—oh—oh.

Bright sparks flared along the pathway between their minds, sizzling with a vivid blaze of gold and red. She grabbed ahold of it and did as he'd asked, fused the link fully into place at both his end and hers, ensuring their merged connection could never be severed, not by either of them. Tears misted her gaze. They'd joined together in the most elemental way, and never had she felt so very full and complete, both body and mind.

"Did I hurt you?"

"Aye, a little, but all will be well. Keep moving." Hungry for more, she sucked on his lower lip, nipped it between her teeth then moaned as he bucked inside her. A low rumble vibrated against her chest as he rubbed against her. More, she needed even more and he delivered.

He caught her mouth with his and liquid heat surged through her core as he rocked over top of her, pulled back then heaved all the way back in again. Moving swifter and deeper with each powerful stroke, he pounded into her and brought such pleasure to her very soul. This bond was magical, beyond enchanting and now all theirs.

"Again," she demanded and he lunged in, filled her completely and she clung to him, her arms wrapped tightly around his neck as he thrust over and over, his cock driving into her with such a heavenly force. Unadulterated pleasure coursed through her, more than she could hold onto.

"Sorry, my love, but I need you, now." He pumped into her, and her channel tightened, her need as great as his. She squeezed his cock ruthlessly and as she did, his essence shot from him in one long, hot spurt. It coated her womb and she catapulted

toward a peak, flew from the very top and soared straight over the edge, her chosen one's thoughts swirling possessively in and around her own. Pure heat and pleasure roared through his mind, just as it did her own.

She would be his bride from this moment forth, until the very end of time. Their mated bond one that none could ever severe, not a single soul. She'd never allow it.

* * * *

Still half insane with need, Ronan held himself perfectly still as he rested deep inside Kyla. When she'd shared all her thoughts and desires along their merged connection, he'd no longer been able to hold himself back and he'd buried himself fully and deeply inside her. Her wicked heat and heavenly warmth had saturated him, her channel so perfectly tight.

Gently, he captured her full breasts in his hands and eased them together. He hadn't spent nearly enough time worshiping these two beauties, an omission he needed to rectify, now.

He rolled his tongue around one delectably tight nipple, sucked the treasure deep inside his mouth and groaned as his need for her built to fierce and fiery life all over again. Damn it. He'd hardly gone soft down below and now he was rock hard once more. There would be no leaving the sanctuary of her body yet.

Lavishing her breasts, he nipped and licked as he surged into her. Never had he tasted a more delicious meal than his bride and if he intended on surviving the next few hours then he'd be partaking of all she could offer him, over and over until he'd saturated himself in her. Only then could he ride out as she'd asked. With one palm around the back of her head, he tangled his fingers in her long golden-red locks and kissed her with all the wild need flaring to ravenous life within him. "You're my true mate, the one I'll always hunger for."

"As I will always hunger for you." She caressed down his back and over his backside, her eyes twinkling with such devilment. "I feel so greedy."

"That makes two of us." He kissed her as he slid his cock back out then pushed all the way back inside her again. They fit together with sheer perfection, her body accepting every single inch of his, and with her mind open as she shared her thoughts along their connection, his heart and soul lifted even higher.

"Mmm." Eyelids fluttering closed, she moaned her pleasure, every inch of her hot channel squeezing him to the point of pain, the pressure tightening his balls and making him want to ram into her.

"Am I too heavy?"

"Gloriously so." She licked his bottom lip, nibbled along his jaw then pushed him over and rolled with him until she came up on top. Back arched and her breasts thrust toward him, she edged up until she sat across his hips, his cock still wedged deep inside her as she stretched her arms high above her head.

"I love it when you sit on top of me. This will likely become one of my most favored positions." He glided over her lush breasts, every inch of her an enticement he couldn't get enough of.

"I love being right here too." She wriggled against his groin, her breasts swaying heavy and full and completely demanding his attention.

"You're giving me the most wicked thoughts." He dotted her breasts with love bites before he sucked one nipple deep inside his mouth and swiped the tip with his tongue.

"This one is missing out." She lifted her other breast to him. "It also requires your very special brand of touch."

He bestowed her other breast with the same attention as he'd given the first then grazed a finger through her curls below and fondled her nub.

She squeaked when he did and her breathing quickened. She lifted up and sank back down on him, did so again and again, building a wicked rhythm as she rode him so beautifully.

"Oh goodness. I seem to tingle everywhere, no matter where you touch me."

"If you feel too sensitive, tell me."

"Aye, too sensitive, but I still want more." Whimpering with need, she picked up her pace, her breasts bouncing about and he ran his tongue around each nipple in turn, the aureoles beading tighter and harder.

"I need more of you too." He seized her mouth and kissed her, swept his tongue over hers in a hot caress that sent red hazing behind his eyes. He had to have her, now. He toppled her onto her back and with one fierce stroke, drove deep inside her and she scraped her nails down his back, her possessive touch making him lose all control.

Again and again, he thrust then with one definitive flick of his finger over her nub, she gasped and cried out, her channel pulsing around him and he gave into his need, his essence streaming from him and pumping into her. Sheer love for his woman took ahold of him and saturated his senses. With her in his arms, her heartbeat a pounding mess against his, he reveled in their joining and the deep depths their bond ran.

"Oh, glad I am that this is now your chamber too." She stretched underneath him, the sunlight dancing over her flushed cheeks and lush breasts.

"I would starve if you ever kept me from your bed." Slowly, he eased his rocking and brought them both gently back down. He'd taken her hard, needed to ensure all was well. That desire overrode all else and carefully, he eased out and knelt between her spread legs, glided his hands over her inner thighs and touched the smear of blood streaked across her flesh. Thank heavens he'd found her before she'd ever spoken vows with Duncan. If he'd taken only a few more days to reach her, then he would've been a few days too late, her innocence gifted to another.

"Your thoughts are clear to see along our connection." Her

blue gaze softened. "Dinnae consider what-ifs. You are here, and we are now man and wife. That is all there is to consider."

"Aye, you're right." And he was supposed to be ensuring her care. He shuffled off the bed and crossed to her side table scattered with her personal belongings. He lifted the jug and poured water into the basin, flapped out a clean cloth from the pile and dipped it into the water. "I just wish I'd returned sooner to claim you."

"You came as soon as you could, and I didnae make it easy for you being that I resided deep within the enemy's territory." She stretched where she lay on the bed and he returned to her, nudged her knees farther apart and tenderly wiped her flesh.

"How sore are you?" He cleaned his cock with the cloth, tossed it back into the basin of water where it landed with a splash then bent over his woman and pressed a soft kiss against her mouth. On his side, he lay down next to her, lifted one of her legs and eased it between both of his, wrapped his arm around her waist and drew her closer until every inch of their bodies touched. "I crave being near you."

"I crave this nearness too, and I'm a little sore, as to be expected." Along his hip, she stroked, her sweetly sensual touch bringing such a deep level of satisfaction to his very soul. "Even though I dinnae wish to leave this bed, 'tis morning and I should go and check on Gordon's wounds and ensure all is healing as it should."

"Gordon can look after himself. You're going to remain right here with me. I need an hour's rest afore I must leave." He yawned and closed his eyes, his need for sleep overwhelming him. It had been some time since he'd last been so content and the dark swirled around him as he held his mate safe and secure in his arms. Nowhere else did he long to be, other than right here with her. "Rest," he murmured as he succumbed to sleep himself.

* * * *

Kyla snuggled against Ronan as he slipped into sleep. He'd ridden hard right through the night, not resting at all as she had, and soon must leave. Outside, the clanging of swords ricocheted toward her. Her clansmen trained and even though Ronan had said Gordon could look after himself, she was still responsible for ensuring his wounds healed without any festering. She couldn't rest when that need tugged at her so strongly.

As Ronan's arms went slack around her, she slowly, carefully, snuck out of his hold and stood. Ouch. Muscles she'd never used before ached in protest, although she should have expected such a thing. She was a woman who'd been well and truly loved by her husband. A lazy smile lifted her lips and she hugged herself. This discomfort was one she intended to embrace and cherish.

Tiptoeing to her ambry, she moved with all stealth and eased the golden curtain back. Elegant gowns hung in a myriad of rich colors and fine fabrics. She nabbed a favorite gown and footwear, crept behind her dressing screen and set her things on the stool behind her. Over her head, she pulled on a cream under-tunic with rucked sleeves and slid her sleeveless burgundy gown overtop. The velvet swished over her hips and brushed her ankles. With the ribbons in hand, she tightened the bodice and made a bow at the top of the low-cut neckline embellished with cream crocheted detailing, the same adornment that ran in a long line down the center of her gown to her feet and ringed the hem. Seated on the stool, she tugged her matching burgundy slippers on then ducked over to her side table.

Ronan still slept, having not moved an inch.

She combed and braided her hair, selected a lacy white ribbon from the shell dish overflowing with ribbons and tied the silk at the end. Loose locks wisped free at the side of her face and she curled the strands around her fingers dampened with a little water and left them bouncing free.

Her new ring sparkled, so shiny and bright on her finger,

although 'twas a little big and slipped off and on with ease. Mayhap 'twas best she kept it secure in her wooden keepsake box until the armorer could adjust the band. He honed weapons to perfection, made repairs on all manner of things and had a particular love of crafting trinkets and such. She'd ask him to resize it.

Around the bed, she crept, leaned over her chosen one and touched her lips to his cheek. His lush lips begged to be kissed and she wanted to lick and nibble on them but if she did, she'd wake him and right now she needed to tend to Gordon before she could return to him.

She snuck to the door and without a noise, slid the bolt across and stole outside.

Down the darkened stone passageway with its wooden floorboards and iron wall sconces, she walked, the immense joy in her heart making her want to skip and sing. Her love for Ronan overflowed her heart and never had she felt so alive.

"About time you surfaced." Jeremiah stepped out from within a darkened niche at the top of the stairwell, his fiery red hair brushing his wide shoulders and his expression thunderous. Dirt clung to his green rawhide pants and his black war coat swayed against his legs. Heavily armed, his claymore sat snugly in a baldric across his back and a dagger glinted from where he'd tucked it into one knee-high boot.

"What are you doing here? I—I—how did you get in?"

"I hear you're one of the fae, dear sister, an unskilled one, although you still hold strong fae blood and I want it gracing my own line." His beady black eyes narrowed. "Father told me the truth about you and your abduction and he agreed I could claim you as my bride. 'Tis time for us to get to know one another better."

He shoved her back into the nook and she hit her head on the rough stone wall.

Black dots danced before her eyes. Nay, she had to hold

onto the present.

"Sleep now, lass." Jeremiah thrust an odorous rag over her nose and rasped in her ear, "You'll soon be mine to wed and bed, and I willnae allow you to sway me to any other decision. I will rule over you. Make no mistake about that."

"I—" So woozy. Everything spun, and her legs dropped out from under her.

Jeremiah heaved her up and her belly thumped into his rock hard shoulder, the sedative lacing the cloth one she'd never mistake for any other. Belladonna. She tried to search for Ronan and connect with him along their merged link, to warn him of Jeremiah's arrival, only all went dark and she sank into complete and utter oblivion.

* * * *

Pain slammed though Ronan's chest and he jerked awake, clutched his sword where it sat propped against the headboard and bounded to his feet. He swung his blade within the stillness of the chamber, the light flaring through the window bright and the fire still well ablaze. 'Twas as if someone had struck him through the heart with a sword, the pain of his loss slicing deeply within him. He patted his chest to be sure, then went to reach for Kyla but the bed lay empty.

"Kyla?" He stalked around to her dressing screen. Not there. He marched to her ambry and flung the golden curtain aside. Gowns hung in an assortment of colors, but no Kyla. Surely she hadn't dressed and left without him stirring to the noise? He held the battle skill and as such always maintained an alert state, even when he closed his eyes to rest.

He stormed to the door. The bolt had been pushed back, unlocked from within and only Kyla could have done that. Hell, he must have been beyond exhausted when he'd fallen asleep. Certainly joining with his chosen one had been an incredibly soul-satisfying moment, one that had made him languid and at such ease afterward. He rubbed his head as he tried to open their fused link. He should be able to now it remained a solid pathway either of them could open at will, only nothing but a stark darkness lay where she should be. Only a few things could cause that. If she spoke to another through her skill, if she rested or such, or if she'd chosen to keep him locked out. Since she'd clearly snuck out of their chamber after he'd fallen asleep, that left the last option as the most viable one. Aye, what could his wife be up to that would require such secretiveness, that she'd leave their bed and close her mind to him?

Well, he wasn't having that. He nabbed his bag, swung it on top of the rumpled bedcovers and lifted the flap. Black leather pants in hand, he hauled them on, donned a blue tunic over top and tucked his shirttails in. He no longer needed to wear the MacKenzie kilt, the added protection of blending in now unnecessary since all within this keep would soon know his true name. Duncan had ensured his men here would never harm one of the fae either, which included him and as they'd soon learn, Kyla too. With her marriage to him, her secret would soon be exposed to her fellow kinsmen within these walls.

He pulled his boots on and strapped his sword in place. Time to find his wife. Mayhap she'd gone to check on Gordon, the healer in her too strong to halt. If she had, he'd toss her over his shoulder and march her straight back to their bed. She'd soon learn how deep his need for her ran, her continued protection as well.

"Ronan?" A knock rattled the door. "'Tis Duncan."

"Come in."

Duncan marched inside, his fists clenched as he searched the chamber. "Where's Kyla?"

"I awoke and found her missing, expect she's gone to check on Gordon. I was on my way there now. I've spoken handfast vows with Kyla, must ride out soon to see her parents and procure a priest."

"One of my guardsmen was attacked within the

underground tunnels leading to the dungeons, right at the point where the passageway divides into three. One of the tunnels leads back here to the keep, while the other passageways veer in differing directions, one toward the hills and the other through the forest to the loch's edge. The guard, when he awoke after being hit over the head, reported 'twas Jeremiah who attacked him and he was headed directly toward the keep."

"Jeremiah's aware of the tunnels?" His heart heaved within his chest.

"Aye, but I lengthened the tunnels this past fortnight and changed their positions, ensured each exit point was well covered. Jeremiah must have stumbled upon one of the new entrances by chance. Gordon has also returned to light duties and I have no' seen Kyla, either in her healer's chamber or the great hall. I've men on guard all over this keep, although Jeremiah is a snake, can get in and out of the tightest spots. We must find her, now."

"Ronan! Duncan!" Hamish rushed into the room, his breath coming hard. "Jeremiah has Kyla and he's sailing to Rhue Castle. He sedated her and she remains out to it. I saw all within a vision."

"Damn it." His enemy had stolen his wife right out from under his eyes. "I'll slaughter him. We've spoken handfast vows and there is none who can now dispute we are wed."

"Jeremiah will find a way to dispute whatever he wishes." Duncan growled low under his breath. "Rhue is a highly fortified stronghold that sits in a prime position right on the rocky headland of Loch Broom. There is only one way in, and that's through the main gate."

"I'll never allow Jeremiah to take my wife from me." He nabbed his satchel and sprinted out the door. Duncan and Hamish chased him downstairs and into the inner courtyard. Duncan bellowed to his men to ready the galley and they raced out under the arched gate, bolted down the sea-gate stairs where the waves crashed in hard against the stone landing. Warriors swarmed onto the vessel, stowed their weapons and nabbed their oars. Hell, he should never have fallen asleep without first ensuring his wife understood all the possible threats.

"Listen to me well!" Duncan hollered as he gripped his shoulder. "Ronan is Niall's son and like his father, holds the fae battle skill. He is now also my brother, wed to Kyla. We sail for Rhue Castle to retrieve her from Jeremiah."

The men roared and pumped their fists into the air.

Their agreement to aid him almost brought him to his knees. None here despised him because of his fae blood. To the men, he shouted, "No one imprisons my wife against her will. We'll find her then free her. She is both a Matheson and a MacKenzie, loyal to each and every man afore me."

"All to oars," Duncan ordered as he gripped the sail's ropes and tossed him one.

Together, they heaved the sail up.

Chapter 6

A screeching cacophony assailed Kyla's ears and she blinked her eyes open as seagulls squawked somewhere overhead. Her head pounded as if horses stampeded within and when she touched the back of her head, she grimaced. Such a terribly large lump had swelled forth.

All around her warriors sat on bench seats with oars in hand, stern-faced and wearing the MacKenzie plaid. Swaying, she sat up within the hull, the vessel surging forward over white-capped waves and making her belly roll.

Breathing deep of the crisp sea air, she squinted toward the land up ahead and tried to make some sense out of it all. A rag lay tucked in the bodice of her burgundy gown, half flapping out and reeking of belladonna. Ugh. No wonder everything still spun. She tore the rag out and it flew over the side and got swallowed up by the churning seas.

Directly ahead, a castle sat high on the rocky headland at the entrance to a loch and a range of mountains rose in the distance behind it, sheep dotting the craggy hills. A horn blasted across the bay and at the castle's sea-gate, two burly warriors strode along a stone landing and bounded into the waist-deep water.

"Lower the sail!" A man's bellow came from behind her and she cranked her head around. Jeremiah stood at the stern, an ominous cast of dark clouds gusting behind him and his fiery red hair whipping about his shoulders.

Oh hell. How on earth had she come to be with Jeremiah?

Clarity hit hard and fast and images swirled through her mind. Jeremiah had shoved her into the wall then thrust a cloth over her mouth.

She snarled under her breath. Jeremiah would pay dearly for doing such a thing, for taking her from Carron Castle against her will, and from right under a heavily fortified garrison of her brothers' men.

Pushing to her feet, she wobbled and grasped the center mast to steady herself. Seawater sloshed within the hull and she slapped her wet skirts. The bow rose sharply up and she almost toppled over as they crested a large swell and cruised in toward the sea-gate. The awaiting warriors seized both sides of Jeremiah's birlinn and brought them in closer to the stony landing. Waves crashed into the rocks alongside the bay and spray misted over her. She shivered from the cold, yet the fierce heat of anger roared through her.

"'Tis about time you awoke, lass." Jeremiah strode down the aisle toward her. "A whole day has passed since we left Carron and I thought you intended to remain asleep the entire time. Welcome to Rhue."

"Welcome?" She wanted to spit on him, to rant and rave. "How dare you steal me away from my home and then state words of welcome. You have no right to take me wherever you please."

"I have every right. Our chief has decreed you'll wed me." He planted his booted feet wide. "'Tis of course a shame you remain unskilled, but your fae blood is strong and that is all that matters."

"Duncan is going to kill you. Coll too the moment he

discovers what you've done."

"Neither of them have a choice in the matter. Our father has spoken." Jeremiah hoisted her up, swung her onto the landing and bounded in beside her. Smirking, he crossed his thick arms as his men marched up the raggedy stone stairs ahead of them and streamed under the arched main gate.

This was the last place she wished to be, or left alone with him. "I hate you."

"Aye, we've never seen eye to eye, but that will change. As your husband, I'll expect your complete obedience once we've spoken vows. Certainly should you give yourself to me willingly, then things will go so much easier for you. Choose to be unwilling, and I'll force you to my hand regardless." He gripped her shoulders and turned her toward the castle then slapped her bottom. "Move ahead."

She gasped and stumbled along the walkway. "Cease manhandling me."

"I enjoy a feisty tumble, and I intend for you to be one."

"I truly, truly hate you." Over her shoulder, she shot him a dirty look as she stomped up the trail after his men toward the two-story gatehouse where several guardsmen stood on duty.

"There is a clergyman right here at this keep. Brother John will oversee our vows and following our marriage, you'll give me plenty of sons who we'll raise right here at Rhue. Am I understood?"

"I will never speak vows with you, not when—" Images hazed her mind and she allowed her skill to rise. Her ability soared free and she flew directly toward her chosen one, the pathway to Ronan's mind one she'd never release. She found him, dived deep within his mind and clung to his roiling thoughts. "*I'm here, Ronan.*"

"*Duncan and I are coming. I have no' been able to reach you. What did Jeremiah do to you?*" Fear and anger pummeled through him as he stood in a pair of black leather pants, a billowy blue tunic plastered to his chest and one hand braced against the mast of Duncan's war galley. The square white sail was pulled taut as the vessel cruised alongside Scotland's rugged western coastline. The galley rocked and dipped, the waves slapping against the hull while overhead heavy gray clouds bubbled and brewed, a storm that loomed all around her as well. He was close, very close, on a seaward path heading directly toward her.

"Jeremiah sedated me and I've only just awoken. How did you learn where I am?"

"Hamish had a vision. He saw Jeremiah setting sail for Rhue, with you onboard."

"Jeremiah has made his intentions clear. There's a clergyman here at this keep and he intends for us to wed, for me to give him plenty of sons. I cannae tell him about you afore you've had the chance to send word to my parents. I willnae have their lives placed in danger."

"We'll be there in a matter of hours."

"This is all such a mess. Jeremiah has declared war against my brothers."

"Aye, he has, and me along with them. It's also a war I'll never allow him to win. Look ahead, love, show me everything as you enter Rhue. I need to know every detail."

"Of course." She walked under the main arch, halted in the inner courtyard and slowly turned around, giving him the layout and position of the guards. *"The curtain walls are the thickest I've ever seen and the tower house sits right alongside the wall overlooking the ocean. There is naught but sheer rock everywhere."*

"Duncan and I will find a way to retrieve you, even if we must tear the walls down to do so."

"Secure the keep!" Jeremiah called to his guardsman at the gatehouse. "No one enters, no' a soul. Raise the alert should you see any vessels out at sea. I need to be informed immediately should we have any unwanted visitors, my brothers included amongst them."

"Aye, my laird." The guardsman lowered the portcullis within the stone-arched entrance, its clunky chains clanging and the thundering rumble echoing with finality all around her.

Dread filled her, the cold invading her limbs. Nay, she needed to remain strong, to not show any fear, because Jeremiah would certainly take every advantage of her the moment she did. Ronan was with her, taking each step she did. Across the gravelly inner yard, she walked while the skies above continued to blacken. A warrior lit the torches mounted against the stone walls and the light flickered eerily up toward the battlements. *"Night is about to fall."*

"Duncan and I will use the darkness to our advantage."

"Please, dinnae get hurt." If her mate came to any harm because of her, she'd never forgive herself.

"I'll take every care, but I will get you out of there, however I can."

She stepped through the main doors of the keep and a boisterous buzz of voices echoed toward her. With one deep, fortifying breath, she walked through the foyer and entered the great hall.

The vaulted room held a crown of high wooden beamed rafters, the walls covered with well-crafted tapestries and herbal wreaths. Rushes lay strewn across the floors and the fresh scent of lavender wafted all around. Trestle tables groaned under the weight of the feast laid out for the returning men. Platters of cooked meat, roasted vegetables, and an assortment of pastries and other sweet dishes made her belly rumble with hunger.

Warriors eased onto the wooden benches and serving maids carrying trays holding steaming bowls of seafood stew, weaved around them. There had to be a good eighty warriors in this hall alone, not to mention the score or so on duty outside. *"Jeremiah has around a hundred men."*

"*Even that number will never keep me from you.*"

"Come and meet Fiona." Jeremiah urged her toward the dais where a lass sat at the high table. "Although if I remember rightly, you two already know each other from my father's keep."

Tall and lithe, Fiona held a pale complexion and stunning red locks that tumbled down to her waist, a mass of bright curls she'd never forget. Goodness. It had been a year since she'd last seen her. "*Ronan, do you remember when I spoke to you about Fiona? She holds a touch of fae blood and a weakened skill. She wed a man several years her senior then left for Rhue. She's the one I first created a merged link of the mind with.*"

"*I see her too.*"

Fiona's corseted forest-green velvet gown hugged her slim waist, the rich cream and gold silk ribbons lacing the front an entwining of vibrant colors. "*I need to warn her about all that's happened and why I'm here. I can garner her aid, find out if she knows of a way out of here, but I cannae forge a connection with her without first releasing this link with you.*"

"*Then cut it.*" He growled the words, those clearly the last he wished to utter. "*Be safe, my love.*"

"*I shall.*" She pulled back from Ronan's mind, dropped their connection then bridged the gap between her and Fiona and delved into her friend's mind, the link one of deep familiarity. "*Fiona, 'tis I, Kyla. Glad I am to see you, but I am no' here of my own freewill. Dinnae give my actions away, that I speak to you right now.*"

"*Kyla?*" Fiona's wide-eyed gaze landed on her, shock pounding through, although she quickly hid her surprise. "*What are you doing here, and with Jeremiah no less?*"

"*I shall tell you everything soon, the moment we're alone.*"

"Fiona." Jeremiah waved out to her friend and motioned for her to join them near the base of the stairwell where a warrior in heavy chainmail stood on guard.

Fiona rose from the high table and walked across to them, nodded at Jeremiah. "Welcome home, my laird. I pray you had a safe and swift journey."

"I did." He gestured toward Kyla. "I've brought Mistress Kyla with me. 'Twould have been a while since you've seen her?"

"Aye, a year now, since the day I left our chief's keep." Fiona smiled at her. "Welcome to Rhue."

"Take Kyla to the chamber that connects to mine," Jeremiah continued. "She is now my betrothed and I'm sure she'd like to bathe and eat afore we speak our vows later this evening."

"Of course." Fiona dipped her head then snuck a look at her. "*You have a lot of explaining to do, my friend.*"

To the guard, Jeremiah issued, "You're to remain on duty directly outside my betrothed's chamber and she isnae to leave it, no' one step beyond her door. I shall collect her soon. Am I understood?"

"Aye, my laird." The guard, his dark blue eyes appearing almost midnight-black behind the slits of his nasal helm, towered over her.

"Come with me." Fiona motioned for her to follow her upstairs and the guard clomped in behind them in his heavy chainmail. Fiona slowed on the first landing as a maid walked downstairs toward them. "Meg, I need a bath prepared for the laird's betrothed, within the blue chamber that connects to his. Bring a tray too, and be as quick as you can about it."

"Aye, mistress." The girl dashed back upstairs.

"This way." Fiona guided her the rest of the way to the third floor then down a passageway lit by the odd flickering candle in a wall sconce.

They slowed as up ahead, Meg ushered two lanky lads who heaved a wooden tub between them into a chamber. At the doorway, they waited as the lads set the tub down then shuffled out and raced downstairs, their shirttails fluttering loose over their breeches.

Fiona walked inside and she followed her. Shivering, she rubbed her chilled arms. A large bed with a vivid blue velvet canopy took pride of place against the far wall with a carved wooden trunk sitting at the end.

Meg knelt at the hearth and tore bark from a log, lit the fire and coaxed the sparks into a welcoming blaze of heat. She added a block of peat and as it crackled and caught alight, she rose to her feet, dusted her hands against her aproned skirts and nodded at Fiona. "Is there aught more ye need, mistress?"

"It appears our laird's betrothed has arrived without her belongings so I'll need you to fetch some gowns from my ambry for her, slippers and a nightgown too."

"Of course." The maid breezed through the door and closed it behind her, the guard standing tall and strong in his position across the darkened passageway.

"Thank heavens we're finally alone." Fiona grasped her hands, tugged her toward the bed and plopped down. "Now, tell me all."

"'Tis so good to see you, although I'd rather that had never been here." She sat, took a steadying breath. "Obviously I've no wish to wed Jeremiah. He snuck into Carron Castle then stole me away, cited his father's permission as acceptance in doing so, although Duncan sails to these shores as we speak, my chosen one with him."

"You're mated?" Fiona clasped a hand to her mouth. "Are you certain?"

"Aye, and 'twas a shock to discover a bond had formed between us. His name is Ronan Matheson and he's a warrior from the fae village. Afore Jeremiah abducted me, Ronan and I spoke handfast vows and since my arrival, he and I have spoken along our merged link. He'll be here soon, intends to find a way inside to free me."

"Jeremiah still has no knowledge of your mind-walker skill?"

"Nay, although Colin told him the truth about my fae heritage, that he'd abducted me as a child from the village."

"Jeremiah has always hungered to have fae blood running within his line, has become fixated on it even more of late." Fiona leaned closer. "I'm aware of Coll's mission, that he travels the length and breadth of MacKenzie land in search of more warriors who'll give him their loyalty. Coll sought Jeremiah's hospitality two months past and stayed with us. Coll and I spoke, privately of course, and he told me of Muirin and Hamish, that they now reside at Ardan House. I'll never forget that first night you and I met, when you arrived at the chief's keep with your mama and I snuck into the solar and hid under the table. I'd already sensed something special about Coll and Duncan through my ability, and when I learnt of their fae blood that night, all made so much more sense."

"Where is Matthew?" Fiona's husband too might offer her his aid should she need it, all dependent on how deeply his loyalty to Jeremiah was over Coll and Duncan.

"Mathew is—" Her friend's eyes suddenly filled with tears. "You have no' heard?"

"Heard what?" More dread filled her.

"M-Matthew suffered a nick to his arm during a training session in the yard, the smallest wound, but it festered and he took a fever. He passed away nigh on two months ago, only a few days after Coll left."

"I'm so sorry. I've been at Carron that long and had no' heard. Is your father aware you're without a husband?" Gregor's allegiance to his chief overrode all, but he loved his daughter, wouldn't wish for her to be suffering unnecessarily. She pulled Fiona into her arms, her heart heaving for her dearest friend.

"I asked Jeremiah to send my father a message, of which he did, but then he told my father I had no desire to return. He's such a scoundrel. He has a great interest in my skill even though 'tis a weakened one, far more than our chief ever did. He has even alluded to making me his leman, of which I'll never agree to." Fiona sniffed and wiped her cheeks. "I fear remaining here now Matthew is gone, but I've had no other choice. I do all I can to be pleasant to Jeremiah, even though I detest doing so."

"Then you'll come with me when I escape." Never would she allow her friend to remain here with Jeremiah, not now. "Ronan and Duncan will be here soon and if you no longer have the protection of a husband, then you'll be safe with me at Carron. Duncan will send word to your father from there should you still wish it, and if no' then you'll stay with me."

"I wouldnae wish to be a burden." Such hope bloomed in Fiona's eyes. "Are you certain I can remain with you?"

"You would never be a burden, and all is settled. You're coming with me, whether I must drag you along or no'."

A knock sounded.

"That'll be the maid." Fiona hugged her, a smile lifting her lips. "I'll come, as well as try to find a way out of here for us." She walked to the door and opened it, bid the servants who'd returned to enter.

Two maids in brown kirtles and two lads hustled forward, each carrying a steaming pail of water. Meg swept inside too, garments draped over her arm. The maid bustled across to the ambry and hung the gowns and a lacy white shawl before setting a folded white shift on the end of the bed next to her. Another lass entered with a tray and placed it on the side table, while Fiona busied herself overseeing the filling of the tub. Her friend added a few drops of scented oil and the sweet aroma of vanilla swirled through the steamy air and filled the chamber with its familiar scent.

Once the servants had filed out, Fiona shut the door and patted the chair in front of the table. "You must be hungry after your journey and this meal is warm and hearty, will fill your belly well. Eat, replenish your strength, for we have quite the night ahead of us.”

“I am famished.” She’d eaten naught in well over a day and her hunger and thirst beat at her. A meal and a hot bath would be most welcome, particularly while she considered her next move. She sat and poked her nose over the bowl of chunky beef stew, breathed deep of the rich scent of the steaming meat and hearty vegetables. “This smells heavenly, no matter I’m currently in the least heavenly place of all. Finding you here though, proves I was meant to come, even under the circumstances in which I did.”

“Aye, your arrival is a blessing in disguise.”

“More than blessing, no’ that my chosen one will see that as the truth right now.” With a slice of crusty bread in hand, she dipped it into the stew and took a hearty bite. The flavors danced across her tongue and warmth raced to her belly.

“Honestly, you are the hope I’ve been praying for since I lost Matthew.” Fiona perched on the dark blue and white padded corner chair. “Tell me more about Ronan, your mate. What’s he like?”

“Ronan holds the battle skill as Coll and Duncan do, even sensed the bond forming between us twenty years ago, afore I was abducted from the fae village.” She dunked her spoon into the stew and sipped from it. “A month ago when Ronan and I first met, ’twas unfortunately no’ under the best of circumstances. Duncan had captured him and his father, Niall, imprisoned Ronan within Carron’s dungeons and taken Niall onto Ardan House. ’Tis a long story, and one I will surely spill all the details about another time, but while Ronan was chained within Carron’s cells, I tended him and that was when I first touched his mind and he sensed my presence. I should have known better than to do so. Mama had warned me never to touch the mind of another holding fae blood, that they could so easily sense my presence if I did, but I just couldnae help myself with

Ronan."

"Never could you have turned your chosen one away."

"Aye, and thankfully he saw through my stubborn stand against him, only no' long after his arrival he escaped and after healing from his injuries, returned to claim me. I've never been so happy as I have since he did."

"As a wee lass, I always dreamed of holding such a soul bound connection, had hoped since I held a fae skill that I might. Of course, 'twas never to be." Another tear trickled down Fiona's cheek as she plucked a thin strip of black leather free from under her bodice and rubbed a ring swinging from the center between her thumb and forefinger. "I loved Matthew, but we didnae have long together."

"You've barely been given time to grieve and that isnae good for you." She sipped wine from her goblet. "You'll be able to do so at Carron."

"One cannae show too much weakness here." Fiona crossed to the tub, knelt and swirled her hand through the water. "This is the perfect heat. Come and bathe afore the water gets cold."

"One moment." She finished her stew then on her feet, unlaced the front stays of her burgundy gown, wriggled her hips and allowed the velvet to slither to her feet. With the cream under-tunic hauled over her head and damp slippers kicked off, she stepped into the tub and sank into the water. Down, she dunked, head and all then emerged and picked up the bar of soap the maid had left beside the tub. She worked the soap into a lather and with vanilla scented suds in hand, washed her hair while Fiona paced before the crackling fire. "How goes your empath ability, Fiona?"

"Since Matthew and I arrived here I've sensed naught but evilness in this place. Certainly a deep bitterness brews within Jeremiah, which became even more obvious when Coll arrived and sought his hospitality. At times I could barely breathe through the resentment bubbling from him. Jeremiah detests the way Colin sent him to his mother's MacLennan clan to be fostered, all while favoring Coll and Duncan and allowing them to remain at Loch Alsh with him. 'Tis why he sailed to see his father this week, to confront him about it all."

"He did, that confrontation ending in his discovery about me. I fear one day Jeremiah will learn the truth about Coll and Duncan's birth as well, then all hell will surely break loose." She more than feared it.

"I fear such a thing too." Fiona shuddered, her hands twisting together. "Jeremiah certainly detests being the third-born son, and even though Coll and Duncan were born from a handfast marriage, Jeremiah would still take every advantage of that and attempt to overthrow them."

A chilling horn shrilled outside and Fiona hurried to the window, her red locks streaming behind her as she flung the shutters open and wedged sideways out to get a better look.

"What is it?" Out of the tub, she splashed, wrapped a drying cloth around her and dashed to her friend's side. Beyond the window, the darkened night skies churned and thunder rumbled somewhere out at sea.

"The point watchman has raised the alert, the signal that a vessel approaches Rhue. One blast means 'tis only a passerby, two blasts for the enemy."

"Then let us hope for a second blast, for my chosen one will never be my enemy, only my very salvation."

* * * *

Ronan joined Duncan where he sat at the stern, the stormy black clouds high above obliterating the stars and allowing only a sliver of the moon to peek through. Thunder boomed and lightning slashed the skies while up ahead, the entrance to Loch Broom rose as they cruised toward Jeremiah's stronghold on the headland overlooking the western coastline of the mainland. Their sea crossing had taken far longer than he wished and as they rounded the point, a horn sounded with one long and eerie blast, then a second shrilled even louder.

"Our arrival has been noted, no' that I expected otherwise." Duncan adjusted the rudder, his gaze narrowed on the stretch of rugged shoreline and the boulders surrounding the sea-gate landing. "Rhue Castle is impenetrable, has never fallen to another. It might be best if we begin by asking Jeremiah to honor the Highland code of hospitality, to request lodging for the night and pray he takes the bait."

"What if he does no'?" Ronan plucked his satchel out from under the bench seat and removed his steel-studded war coat, shrugged it on and lifted the collar higher over his neck. "Are you prepared for a battle?"

"Always, yet I am still his elder brother and if Jeremiah has laid even one finger on my sister, I'll skewer him where he stands."

"Then you'll need to get in line behind me since I intend to skewer him first."

"Ronan?"

"I'm here. Duncan and I have arrived." He straightened on the seat, Kyla's presence in his mind easing a touch of his anxiety. The castle's massive stone walls rose out of the misty dark with forbidding height into the night sky, the windows lit by candlelight and his chosen one ensconced somewhere deep within that stronghold. *"How did your conversation with Fiona go?"*

"Fiona wishes to leave with me. She's widowed now, has been these past two months and has no desire to remain behind."

"Then we'll take her with us." To Duncan, he muttered, "Kyla speaks to me along our merged link. Fiona wishes to leave too, is now widowed."

"Fiona and Kyla used to follow Coll and I around constantly as children. Fiona's a spritely lass and due to her empath ability, has a great deal of love to give. Certainly never a day passed that I didnae catch her sneaking food from the kitchens for a hungry child. She also tended the wounds of our injured kinsmen, right alongside Kyla." Duncan searched the rocky entrance where the waves splashed in hard against the boulders and sprayed high. "We willnae leave either of them behind when we leave."

"Duncan is in agreement with me. Fiona comes."

"Wonderful. I'll speak to you again soon. I must tell her the good news." Their connection dropped away and he sighed with frustration.

"Jeremiah and his guards come!" Hamish bellowed from the bow.

"Have you 'seen' aught more?" Ronan stormed down the center aisle, Duncan right behind him.

"Naught, and 'tis most frustrating." Fisting one hand over the hilt of his belted sword, Hamish growled under his breath. "The moment I have a vision, I shall inform you both."

"How do we explain my close resemblance to Coll?" He eyed the procession of heavily armed warriors marching down the grassy trail toward the sea-gate, Jeremiah at the head. His adversary halted on the stone landing in his rawhide pants and steel-studded black coat, his legs planted wide and his claymore strapped within a baldric across his back. Jeremiah's men took their positions at his flank, all except for two who jumped into the water as their galley crested a wave and sailed in.

"You need to be Rand MacKenzie once more." Duncan clapped a hand on his shoulder. "My brother would certainly have to be blind no' to notice the similarity and he'd question it if I said you were a Matheson. That I cannae have."

"Then Rand I shall be." He had no issue with Duncan's choice and as they neared the landing, Jeremiah's two men gripped the sides of their vessel and brought them up against the sea-gate.

Duncan jumped onto the stony platform and stormed toward Jeremiah.

Ronan bounded from the galley and followed. He'd never allow his cousin to stand alone, not in any way.

"I come in peace, Jeremiah, unlike you did to my shores," Duncan snarled, his war coat flapping against his legs. "I ask for your hospitality this night. We've traveled far and all to ensure Kyla's safe arrival."

"Hospitality?" Jeremiah snorted and shook his head, his red hair gleaming under the torchlight one guard held behind him. "Dinnae try any trickery with me, Duncan. Kyla holds fae flood and you and Coll have had your chance to wed her, could so easily have done so while she was with you at Carron. You can be assured I will make her my wife, that I have our father's permission to do so as well. This night she'll be mine."

"She'll never be your wife." Fury slammed into Ronan and he shoved forward, wanted to wrap his hands around Jeremiah's neck and wring it.

"Stand down, Rand." Duncan hauled him in behind him and Ronan gritted his teeth and forced his hands to remain at his sides. Aye, stand down he would. They needed to secure Jeramiah's hospitality, to get inside those walls if possible.

"My, my." Jeremiah narrowed his gaze on him. "Why is it you look so very similar to Coll, even more so than his own twin does?"

"Rand is one of my most trusted men." Duncan stepped nose to nose with Jeremiah. "I demand to see Kyla and I willnae be leaving here until I've done so."

"I'll never permit you entry into my keep, but if you insist on seeing her then I'll have her brought to the ramparts, right after she and I have spoken our vows." Jeremiah gestured toward the battlements up high where a good score of warriors stood guard. "If you wish, I'll even consummate our union while you watch on, then you'll know for certain she's my wife, and that you'll never get her back."

Pure rage burned through Ronan and Duncan shot him a

look of warning over his shoulder. Never had he been so angry, yet this was exactly what Jeremiah wanted, to taunt and tease them, and if he succumbed to the man's goading, then one wrong move would see him lose the chance to get inside that stronghold to reclaim his bride. He wanted her returned to him, and he wanted her back now. Only careful thought and planning would see that done.

"Be gone with you all." Jeremiah flicked a hand at them as he backed away. "You're to leave the moment you've seen Kyla on the battlements, or else I will carry out my threat and flip her skirts afore you. That I give you my word on."

"No clergyman will ever wed you to Kyla, no' when she must still do so of her own free will and I know my sister well. She will never utter vows with you." Duncan spat on the ground. "Touch Kyla in any way, and I'll gut you with my sword. That I give you my word on."

"Strong words, brother, but meaningless all the same." Jeremiah gave them his back, his warriors closing in behind him as he marched up the sea-gate stairs and inside, the portcullis clanking into place once all were well within.

"I want to do more than gut him." Ronan paced back and forth along the landing. To Duncan's men surrounding him, he muttered, "Make yourselves busy along these rocks. Scatter about as if you're stretching your legs or whatever else comes to mind. I willnae be leaving here without my wife, which means we must find a way inside, and damn soon."

"Follow his order, as if it were my own." Duncan motioned to his men to move out then eyed Hamish. "Tell me you 'see' something."

"No' as yet, but I'll be waiting and watching."

"As will I." Ronan bounded onto the rocks and crouched in the dark, his chest aching and his frustration burning fierce and hot. Find a way in, he would. Or perish trying. There was no other choice.

Chapter 7

Kyla's heartbeat thumped as she stood beside Fiona at her window. "I'll no' wait idly by for Ronan and Duncan to attempt a rescue. We have to find a way out of this place afore my chosen one loses all reason."

"The only way in and out is through the main gate."

"What about from the top of the tower? Can we get upstairs, sneak through the window and use a rope to scale down?"

"Should we fall then we'd end up a bloody mess on the rocks." Fiona closed the shutters over the window. "What of your fae skill? 'Tis said those with the mind-walker ability can sway another's intentions when within their mind. Has your skill ever grown to that level?"

"I've never attempted—oh." Memories surged, of the time when she'd been down in the dungeons with Ronan following his initial capture at Duncan's hands and she'd unknowingly used force against him when she'd issued her command for him to eat. His words flowed through her mind.

"Cease using force against me." He'd taken a hearty swallow of the water, her mind entrenched within his. *"I can sense your fae skill, your subtle yet clear push within my mind to*

make me obey your orders."

"I have no idea what you speak of." She truly hadn't at the time, having never used force before.

"Trust me, you hold a fae skill whether you wish to acknowledge it or no', although it likely lays buried somewhat inside you since you have no' had the chance to be guided by our people in the full use of it. I too am part fae and can sense your ability."

She grinned and cleared her thoughts. "Fiona, I've used force once afore. I'll try to do so again."

"Good, then dress and we'll be away."

She tossed her drying cloth aside and donned the shift the maid had left folded on the end of the bed. From the ambry, she whipped out a gown of the darkest color, one which would aid her in blending in with the night. With the mountainous folds of blue-black fabric in hand, she eased the velvet over her head and the layers slithered down her body and brushed the polished floorboards. Front laces pulled together and tied, she slid her feet into the slippers the maid had brought then ran her fingers through her damp locks. "I'm ready."

"Then we leave, now." Fiona looped one arm through hers and tugged her toward the door.

With one last deep breath to firm her resolve, she stepped into the passageway and with as much force as she could muster, thrust inside the guard's mind. *"I wish to leave, along with Fiona, and you will offer us your aid, immediately. Am. I. Understood?"*

"Aye, my lady." A haze clouded the guard's dark blue eyes through the slits in his helm.

"I—I—" Fiona stared at her in astonishment. "Demand something more. Ask him his name."

Within the guard's mind, she issued, *"Give me your name."*

"Cedric," he mumbled, his gaze still cloudy.

"Oh, that's perfect." Fiona clapped. "Keep doing what

you're doing."

"Cedric, listen to me well. What is the best route for us to get outside, without anyone being any the wiser?"

"The servants' stairwell winds down to the kitchens." Eyes still hazed. "There is a back door in one of the storage rooms that leads to a small rear courtyard."

"Show me the way."

"Of course." He tramped down the darkened passageway then opened a door within a shadowed nook, one she hadn't even noticed on her way up.

"I should have considered the servants' stairwell myself." Fiona hurried through the door Cedric had opened, her forest-green skirts swishing about her.

"Follow me, as quietly and quickly as you can," she issued to Cedric as she rushed after Fiona. Oh goodness. The servants' stairwell was so cramped and dark, lit only by a single candle on the landing just below them. Hands bunched in her skirts, she negotiated the tight turn of stairs with Cedric stooped over behind her. His shoulders brushed the gritty stone walls and his head scraped the low beamed ceiling. Musty air clogged her airways and she fought to drag in each breath.

"We're almost there," Fiona whispered from below as she hurried down the last few steps then halted next to a heavy wooden door and touched the knob. "The kitchens lie right beyond this door."

"Allow me to see." She shuffled past Fiona and creaked the door open an inch. A serving maid bustled about the steamy kitchens and another lass scrubbed pots at the basin. A fire burned in the ovens and the aroma of fruit tarts wafted through the air.

Another maid hustled in, her hands stained red by some kind of berry. She removed the fruit tarts from the ovens, set them on two trays, handed one to the closest maid and picked up the other tray herself before the two of them walked out the door with the pastries in hand.

She closed the door with a *snick* and caught Fiona's hand. "There's one maid remaining, whom we need to get past. Do you think you can get her to leave without raising any questions?"

"I could."

"Or I could." Raspy words from Cedric. He removed his helm and scrubbed a hand through his short black hair lying hot and slick against his scalp, his blue gaze now clear.

Damn it. She no longer held any control over him, had somehow allowed it to slip free.

She nabbed ahold of his mind again and he held up a staying hand, his gaze narrowed. "Nay," he uttered. "You dinnae need to make any more demands of me, or force me to your will. I am of more use to you with my thoughts as my own." He lowered his voice to a whisper. "Coll has my allegiance, given to him during his recent visit. I remain in Jeremiah's stronghold for one reason only, to keep an eye on Coll's wayward brother. I listened in at the door while you both spoke. I too hold a touch of fae blood and Coll has always known that. I am at your service, will always remain loyal to our clan's next chief." He removed his wrist dagger and handed it to her hilt first. "'Tis time for the fae to live."

"You're truly loyal to Coll and Duncan?"

"Aye, the fae blood I hold is four generations removed, and although I hold no skill, my younger sister does. The path I've chosen in joining your brothers' cause is to ensure my sister's future. She shouldnae have to live in fear of Colin or Jeremiah and their devious desires."

"I believe you, and call me Kyla. All my friends do." She pushed Cedric's offered dagger back toward him. "Please, you must help Fiona and I get safely away. That is all I ask of you."

"Once I dispense with the maid, I'll see you directly to the sea-gate entrance myself. Few are aware of it, but there's a deep underwater tunnel that flows from the sea-gate into the keep, one a solitary man can swim through, provided he know where it lies. I do."

"What are you suggesting?" She brushed a cobweb from her arm.

"You both need to be prepared for a swim. I'll sneak you out of here myself through that tunnel."

"Well, 'tis a lovely night for a swim." She grinned at Fiona. "Wouldnae you say?"

"Absolutely."

"Then wait right here while I see to the maid." Cedric eased past them in the cramped space, flung the door open and closed it to within an inch.

Nose to the inch gap, Kyla held her breath.

Cedric strode to the lass and ordered, "The laird's betrothed needs more clothing. Find the seamstress and have her take bolts of cloth to the blue chamber."

"Aye, right away." The lass rushed out the door.

Kyla bounded into the kitchens and hurried to Cedric's side, Fiona one step behind her. "How quickly will she find the seamstress?"

"The seamstress left earlier this eve for the village five miles to the south. The lass will take some time to run that errand. Follow me. I'll no' lead you astray." He walked into the storage room set to the side, opened a tiny door that creaked terribly then closed it after them as they all snuck outside.

In the dark of the night, the fresh sea air swirling all around, they flattened themselves to the keep's stony wall, just out of the sight of the guardsmen patrolling the battlements high above. Cedric edged along until they reached a small nook where stones surrounded a fish pond sloshing with water and the odd lily pad floating on top. He knelt, removed several rocks from around the edge and murmured, "This is where the sea-gate's underwater tunnel begins. It leads directly outside to the rocks near the landing."

"Oh, how clever." She never would have guessed a tunnel lay directly below them.

"I'll go through first, discover Duncan's exact position on the other side of the wall then return for both of you." He rose to his feet. "I overheard you say you hold a merged link with your chosen one. Reach for him along it. Tell him I'm coming."

"Of course." In the future she'd need to take great care if a guard stood outside her door, that he couldn't overhear her, although Coll had already told Cedric the truth, which meant her brother trusted this man implicitly. Since Coll did, so too would she. She opened her link, followed the pathway to Ronan's mind and sank into sheer mayhem when she did, his thoughts a tangled and frustrated mess. "*I have good news.*"

"*Speak it.*"

"*Fiona and I have found a guard who gave his allegiance to Coll during his visit here two months past. Cedric holds a touch of fae blood, even has a sister with a skill. He aids us now.*"

"*Are you certain of his loyalty? This could be a trap set by Jeremiah in the hope of capturing us and bringing your rescue to an end.*"

"*I'm certain, and we've made our way outside via the servants' stairs and are standing within a quiet nook where few tread. Where are you?*"

"*Along the rocks near the sea-gate, discussing exactly how Duncan and I will make our way in. Hamish has seen naught yet, unfortunately.*" A sliver of moonlight streaked through the stormy, darkened clouds above and she looked through his eyes and found him crouched with Duncan, the sea crashing in and spraying over them, a coiled rope and grappling hook in his hands.

"*The guards will be able to see you should you scale the curtain wall, whether 'tis dark or no'. Jeremiah will be awaiting just such a move so he can attack without any recrimination.*"

"*We're well aware, but we have little choice. I'm no'*

leaving here without you. You're my wife and where you are, is where I need to be."

"I will never allow any harm to come to you because of me." She grasped Cedric's mail-clad arm. "Ronan and Duncan are on the rocks next to the sea-gate landing. They're close."

"Tell them to stay right there. I'll come to them." He laid his helm on the ground then removed his chainmail, weapons, and chunky boots. Standing in only his leather pants and black tunic, he snuck his dagger from his wrist sheath and murmured, "I need to ensure the tunnel is clear of any seaweed and debris afore I allow either of you any entry. Disrobe as you can. The current will be strong so the less you're wearing, the better."

"That we can do." She loosened the front stays of her gown and shoved the velvet down before slinking back farther into the darkened shadows in her white shift. *"You must stay where you are, Ronan. Cedric is coming to you through an underwater tunnel that leads directly outside."*

Beside her, Fiona removed her forest-green gown and rolled it into a tight bundle, her brown shift blending in well with the dark.

"Here, you'll need this." Cedric hauled his black tunic off and handed it to her. "Your shift will be a bright beacon out on the rocks. Don my tunic instead. It should reach to your knees."

"Thank you."

"Give me a few minutes. Wait right here for my return." Hunkered down, he removed an iron grate from under the lily pads and carefully propped it against the wall, rolled his pants to his knees and sat on the edge of the hole. Water sloshed as he maneuvered himself down, the rim barely wide enough to allow him to fit through. "Keep to the shadows and dinnae draw any attention to yourselves."

"Of course and there is something I must tell you." She knelt next to him. "Ronan looks eerily like Coll, so you should find him with ease. Take care as you swim."

"I shall." Shoulders scrunched, he sank and disappeared within the murky dark. Bubbles rose to the surface then nothing.

She pulled his tunic on and underneath it, shimmered out of her shift and tucked it within her gown and set her bundle next to Fiona's clothing behind the grate.

"This is probably no' the best time for me to remind you of this"—Fiona clasped her shaking hands together, her bottom lip wobbling—"but I'm still no' overly fond of tight spaces clogged with water, no' since that time we went swimming in the loch and I dove down deep and my foot got trapped between two rocks. You remember that day, dinnae you?"

"Aye, but 'twas so long ago. You must set that fear aside." She scanned the courtyard and shrank back even farther into the shadows against the wall. "Coll and Duncan freed you without any issue that day, and I'll be with you in the tunnel."

"I had to hold my breath for a very long time afore they did." One deep frown.

"I can take ahold of your mind and force you to my will if you wish." She squeezed Fiona's fingers. "Is that permissible?"

"Nay, dinnae do that." Fiona blew out an unsteady breath. "You're right. I must set this fear aside."

"Cedric is here." Ronan's reassuring words resounded in her mind.

"Cedric is with Ronan." She hugged Fiona. While within Ronan's mind, she followed his movements. He shucked his boots, war coat and fur vest, dumped them into Duncan's waiting hands then in his black leather pants and billowy blue tunic, dove into the choppy waves and joined Cedric bobbing in the near dark.

The two sank down, groped for the tunnel's entrance in the murky black then pushed through the tight hole and swam toward them.

"They're both coming." She dropped to her knees, grasped the edge of the rim and searched the watery depths.

Seawater poured over her feet then Cedric emerged, clambered out, his dagger pinched between his blue lips and water sluicing to his feet.

"*Ronan?*" More water gushed.

"*I'm right here.*" He surged out of the tunnel, hoisted himself to his feet and wrapped her up in his chilly embrace.

"I cannae believe you're truly here." She cupped his face in her hands, touched the dark circles rimming his eyes. "I'm sorry. I never meant to cause you such fear and worry."

"Now I've got you back, I'm never letting you go again."

"I shall hold you to that promise." She drew his face to hers and—

"Fiona and I will go first." Cedric sheathed his weapon at his wrist, picked Fiona up and lowered her into the hole then dropped down after her. The two disappeared.

"Kyla." Ronan scooped her up and dangled her feet over the watery hole. "Are you ready to go?"

"As ready as I've ever be."

"I'll be behind you every step of the way." He touched his lips to hers and oh, sweet heaven. One taste of the warm recesses of his mouth was all it took to cloud her senses. She swept her fingers into his hair, clutched him closer, her heartbeat a pounding mess as she kissed him with all the desperate desire she'd held at bay since their parting.

"*Sorry, love.*" He broke their kiss, anguish flaring in his gaze before he dropped her into the hole and icy water closed in over her head.

"*I'll get you back for that.*" She sank into the darkened depths and once her feet touched the stony base, she maneuvered around in the rounded basin then kicked off toward the sea-gate.

* * * *

Releasing Kyla had nearly killed Ronan. With a splash, she'd gone down then he'd given her long enough to turn around within the basin below then feet first, jumped in after her and sank. Holding and kissing his mate was all he desired, not a torturously cold swim through the murky depths of an underwater tunnel on enemy soil.

In fast pursuit, his mind connected with hers, he kicked after her, the high tide swelling and pushing against him. Not much farther. Seaweed swirled all about and he brushed Kyla's bare feet. She too struggled to move forward against the incoming tide and he pushed against her soles and propelled her through.

Once clear of the tunnel, he clutched ahold of her around the waist and heaved them upward through the twisting current. He broke the surface, the waves crashing over them and tossing them about, the sky a welcoming blanket of black with not even a glimmer of the moon in sight.

Hands cinched on her hips, he held her above the water as she gulped in air. "Are you all right?"

"I am now that I have you c-close again." She shivered, her teeth chattering and her long golden tresses snagged around his shoulders. He wanted to wrap the rest of her around him, only he was out of time.

"Let's get you to the galley and warmed up." He kicked toward the slick rocks, hoisted her up into Duncan's waiting arms then seized the hand of one of the other warriors and got pulled out. Water sluiced to his feet as the waves batted the rocks. One of Duncan's men bundled Fiona in a plaid and the warrior bounded across the rocks with her toward their moored vessel.

"I'll do my best to hide your leaving." Cedric bobbed in the rushing surf. "Travel safely."

"Jeremiah will know they had help getting out." He held out his hand to the man who'd brought his chosen one safely back to him. "Neither of the ladies could've lifted that grate propped against the wall. Should you return, it'd be to a certain death. Come with us."

"Please, Cedric." Kyla scrambled out of Duncan's hold and tried to reach for Cedric too. "You must come, and that's an order."

"An order I wholeheartedly agree with." Duncan swamped Kyla in a tartan and covered her from head to toe. "'Tis time for the fae to live, which includes you, Cedric."

"Then I'll come." Cedric gripped Ronan's offered hand and he heaved the warrior out.

"Glad you could join us." He clapped the man's shoulder, scooped Kyla from Duncan's hold and with her bundled up in his arms, rushed across the rocks just as the moon broke free of the stormy clouds.

A horn trumpeted and the blast echoed across the bay. An arrow whizzed through the air and *thunked* into the slick stone at his feet. He bounded into the galley and dashed to the stern.

"Raise your shields and all oars!" Duncan bellowed as he leapt aboard, his men piling in around them.

"Put me down. You need to take cover too." Kyla squirmed in his arms as he rolled her underneath the bench seat where Fiona had already been stashed then covered both their bodies with his.

"Stay still, both of you." More arrows slammed into the hull, one grazing his leg as the vessel heaved over the cresting waves.

"Hamish, take out the archers!" Duncan grabbed the ropes and hoisted the sail. It caught the wind and sent them flying out of the bay.

"What's going on?" Kyla fisted his tunic from behind.

"Wait a moment." He plucked an arrow that had pinned his leather pant leg to the hull, snapped it in two and tossed it before heaving out from under the bench and onto his haunches. At the sea-gate, two birlinns loaded with men sunk lower into the water and shouts echoed. Chaos reigned and Jeremiah's warriors bounded back onto the landing.

"I cannae wait any longer." Kyla scrambled out and peered around him. "Why isn't Jeremiah making chase?"

"Duncan had a couple of our men loosen a few very importantly placed planks on their birlinns just afore I dove into the tunnel to come to you, at Hamish's insistence. 'Twas all Hamish had 'seen,' so we acted on it." He chuckled, his relief immense, the seer's aid exactly what they'd needed. "Jeremiah will have to effect repairs otherwise sink to the bottom of the bay. Chasing us now is impossible."

"Oh, that's so very clever." She bounced about and laughed. "Come out, Fiona. All is clear."

The lass with red hair plastered to her head beamed as she crawled out and skipped in a circle around them. "I cannae believe we're free."

"Aye, and never to return to Rhue again." Kyla grasped Fiona's hands and danced with her.

"I must thank Duncan as well." Fiona giggled and dashed down the aisle.

"As I must thank you." Cheeks pink and blue eyes bubbling with life, his chosen one wrapped her arms around his neck and swayed against him. "Of which there are so many ways I wish to do so."

"And as I certainly wish to be thanked." He took her with him as he sat on the rear seat, tucked her securely on his lap and kissed her until he had no breath left in him.

"Oh my," Kyla panted against his lips. "I adore your kisses."

"I love you." He snatched the tartan that had fallen from her and tucked it more securely around her, tipped her chin up and kissed her all over again. Holding her close, his heart lifted and soared free.

"I love you too, Ronan Matheson." She snuck one hand under the hem of his damp blue tunic and with wandering fingers, trailed over his thumping heartbeat and the hard planes of his belly.

"You're my heart, the other half of my soul, my everything and all." He rocked her in his arms, closed his eyes and reveled in the moment, his chosen one snuggled deep within his mind and her presence bringing such peace to his very soul.

Chapter 8

Waves slapped against the galley's sides and the boat rocked and dipped, the movement and sound pulling Kyla toward wakefulness, a very good and contented wakefulness. Held protectively in her mate's arms throughout the night, she'd fallen asleep and nowhere else did she long to be other than right here with him.

"Go back to sleep." His voice floated over her, his lips brushing her cheek and his body surrounding hers. "Sleep."

"I'm no longer tired." Stretching, she wriggled upright and pushed her eyes open. The skies had lightened, the night having fallen away and the new day's rising sun glimmered along the horizon. Beautiful pinks and yellows speared bright through the pale blue. Scotland's rugged western coastline lay to their left while to their right the blue-green waters held a long line of land rising from it. The northernmost tip of the Isle of Skye. "We're almost halfway home. We've made good time."

"Aye, that we have, and with no sign of Jeremiah."

"Even better." Grinning, she surveyed those on deck. Her MacKenzie clansmen sat on the seats, the odd one snoozing across a bench, while above them the square sail was pulled taut by the brisk breeze. She cupped Ronan's stubbly jaw and he lifted his face to the wind and eyes closed, breathed deep. She did the same, taking in Scotland's freshest air and the scent of pure freedom. Aye, that freedom was now all hers, as well as Fiona's.

"Red Point lies ahead. To shore we go!" Duncan stood at the bow and winked at her, his dark hair blowing in the wind as he stood in command of his vessel. Her brother loved sailing these seas, had always been more at home on the water than he'd ever been on the land. "We'll stretch our legs, eat, and catch a few hours' rest. Sound good, little sister?"

"Oh, aye." She'd dearly love the reprieve from being at sea, that's if she could secure some adequate clothing rather than just this borrowed tunic from Cedric. Halfway up the aisle, Fiona sat clothed in baggy brown breeches tightened around her waist with a leather belt and a billowy white shirt overtop. Borrowed clothes from one of the men.

"Are you hungry?" Kisses feathered over her brow.

"Mmm, very hungry." Bottom snug in Ronan's groin, she nuzzled into the small V at the neckline of his blue tunic now dried by the wind. She nipped his skin, the taste of him completely intoxicating.

"I meant for food." He wriggled underneath her and groaned. "Hold still, love."

"I cannae hold still." And going by the hardening of the bulge within his pants, he too held a definite hunger for her. She tentatively touched the heaviness of his shaft through the soft black leather and another husky groan rumbled from deep within his chest. "Do you hurt?"

"Immensely, and that part of me has no' ceased aching since you fell asleep in my lap."

"An ache I shall tend to the first moment I can." She rubbed her palm over him some more and nibbled again on his neck, grinned as he growled low a second time.

"Lower the sail and all to oars," Duncan ordered, and not

soon enough for her liking or Ronan's either considering his harried thoughts.

Along the rugged coastline, the forest butted right up to the sea and sunshine bathed the treetops a golden hue. They cruised into Red Point beach, found a clear spot on the sand where the men set up camp, hunted game then roasted their catch over an open fire that sizzled and warmed her through where she sat before it. Her belly rumbled as the succulent aroma of cooked goose and fried fish pervaded the air.

"No' long now." Ronan shrugged on a fur vest and settled in behind her, his legs either side of hers.

She leaned back against his chest, her tartan snugly wrapped around her and the fire's brilliant orange and red flames flickering bright. Never had she been so content, well except for her itchy skin. Salt encrusted the black cloth and it scratched and irritated. "I would dearly love a wash and a change of clothes."

"We can bathe after we've eaten. I've been to this place a time or two afore and there's a small pool of water in the forest which is very private." Gently, he swept her hair to one side then buried his nose against her neck, his touch making her want to rub up against him in every single way. "Your skin is so silky and soft, your hair such a striking shade that it shimmers like burnished gold in the morning light."

"It does?"

"Aye," he purred in her ear. "I want to see your hair spread over my pillow as the sun rises each morning, and your skin, I want to explore every inch of it, day and night." He selected one of the sticks of meat from the fire, set it aside to cool down then once it had, he tore off a chunk and slipped the morsel between her lips. "I intend on beginning that exploration very, very soon. How fast can you eat?"

"I can inhale my food if needed." Giggling, she plucked a piece of meat from the skewer and fed him. "What of my parents?"

"'Twill be best if I send a messenger with a missive for them instead of riding to see them myself. You can add your own words to mine. Just dinnae ask me to leave you right now, no' after all that has occurred." He continued to feed her and as they ate, the other men did the same from where they sat scattered about the beach and along the grassy bank edging the forest.

The galley sat half-beached on the sand and Duncan foraged about onboard, snagged a couple of bags then bounded onto the sand and strode toward her. He set one of the bags at her feet then perched on a low boulder wedged in the reddish-gold grains next to her. "I've borrowed some clothes from my squire and they're in that bag. They should fit you. How do you feel?"

"I'm fine, and I'm also truly sorry that Jeremiah caught me unawares at Carron. He didnae give me the chance to call out a warning."

"Jeremiah will never take you from us again, and the moment we return, I'll ensure the underground tunnels are blocked off completely so that none can ever enter through them again." Duncan chose a skewer and bit the meat off. "With your abduction, Jeremiah has declared war against Coll and I, which means building up our ranks is now of the utmost importance."

"You can include me in those ranks." Ronan tightened his hold around her waist as he eyed her brother. "I've no intention of deserting you and Coll when your need is so great."

"You have my immense thanks." Duncan nodded as he ate. "Glad I am to have you as my brother now, and you can be assured neither my men or I will ever raise arms against a Matheson."

"We have so many lost years to make up for." Ronan extended his hand and Duncan shook it.

"That we do."

"'Tis wonderful to see you two getting along so well." She beamed, her happiness overwhelming her. Having her nearest and dearest right here with her was a dream, and once Coll returned from his mission, even more so.

"I would do whatever it took to make you happy." Ronan dropped a soft kiss on her neck. "Have you eaten your full yet?"

"Most definitely."

"Then let's bathe afore we must set sail." He gripped her waist as he rose and set her on her feet then slung both their bags over his shoulder.

With her tartan wrapped snugly around her, she followed him as he strode along the densely wooded trail into the deeper recesses of the forest. The dampness of the earth and the fresh scent of the tall pines swirled all about. Birds twittered from high in their nests, while small creatures scurried about within the undergrowth. She danced along the trail as Ronan walked a few steps ahead of her. Each stride he took was made with such purpose, his leather pants molded to his tight buttocks and powerful thighs, and as a gentle breeze whispered through the trees, it lifted the hem of his blue tunic underneath his fur vest and gave a glimpse of his golden skin and trim hips.

"We're here." He held up a low branch and she passed underneath it.

"Oh." She gasped at the stunning sight. The clear glistening surface of the small loch reflected the brilliant green and gold foliage of the trees towering all around, the sunshine dappling through in patches. "This is perfect, and so wonderfully private."

They'd finally been granted some time alone and she didn't intend to waste a moment of it. She dropped her tartan, seized the hem of her borrowed tunic and lifted it over her head. Black cotton swished to the ground and barefoot, she bounced toward the water. On the mossy edge, her toes curling into the lush softness, she peeked over her shoulder and beamed at her mate. "Are you coming in?"

"Hell, yes." One low growl as he dropped his sword belt and prowled toward her, his gaze sweeping down the long length of her back then getting stuck on her backside. "You have the most luscious bottom I've ever beheld. Have I ever told you that?"

"Nay." She wiggled her bottom at him. "I'll race you to the other side. Catch me if you can." The loch beckoned and she dove then almost lost her breath at the frigid impact with the water. 'Twas chilly, not that she'd allow that to bother her. Under the water, she kicked then broke the surface and grabbed a decent breath of air. Under she went again. Such pure bliss saturated her. This truly was a most magical—

A hand clamped around her ankle and Ronan dragged her back to the surface.

"I want that bottom of yours in my hands." With the water lapping his bare chest and his golden eyes burning a toe-curling hue, he stroked over her lower cheeks, captured her mouth with his and kissed her, so hungrily, so greedily. "I have my beautiful bride back in my arms once again, safe and well and her creamy skin sliding against mine. This is what I've longed for since the moment you were taken from me. Never again will I allow you far from my sight."

"Aye, I will enjoy having you keep a close eye on me." Fingers digging deep in his slick dark hair, the odd strand of pale blond now poking through, she returned his kiss and devoured him, just as ravenously as he devoured her.

"I need you, Kyla." The clear surface rippled as he scooped her higher against him, his feet touching the base as he walked her backward toward the edge, the cool water lapping her breasts and making her already hard nipples stiffen even further. He caressed her lower cheeks and she rocked against the hard length of his cock prodding into her belly.

"Is this for me?" Between them, she curled one hand around his thick shaft.

"Aye, my body is yours, just as your body is mine." Carefully, he sat her on the embankment, her legs dangling in the water. He tipped her back onto the moss, stroked around her breasts in slow circles and licked his lips. "I've been denied my wife and you hold a feast I shall always crave."

"I adore bathing with you."

"You're my chosen one, always mine." He eased her breasts together and licked each nipple, the hot and heavenly stroke of his tongue making her body heat with a need only he could bring to glorious and full life. "You've enchanted me, Kyla, stolen my will to be anywhere else but here with you."

"You say the sweetest things." She stretched out on the moss, sinking deeper into the lushness of it. "I have no wish to be anywhere else either."

"Now we're together, we remain together." He swirled around the tip of her nipple with his tongue, flicked the hard nub then sucked her nipple deep inside his mouth.

An avalanche of sensations raced through her and she clutched his shoulders and held on.

"Do you know what I want?" He swept her legs apart and eased between them, his gaze searching hers.

"Aye, and I want the same." She shoved her elbows under her and lifted up, traced the ridged bands of muscle lining his stomach, his hard muscles honed like carved stone. His abs bunched under her fingertips and as she moved lower and reached the head of his cock, his shaft saluted her from the water. Such pure joy flooded her. She wrapped her hand around the heaviness of him, fondled the head and glided down to the root. Every inch of him was hers to love and cherish, and she certainly would, for the rest of her life. "I want so much, everything you're willing to offer me."

"I intend on lavishing attention on you, and I've no wish to stop." He tipped her back onto the moss once more, lifted her bottom higher and fully exposed her to his ravenous gaze. "My mouth waters at just the sight of all I'm about to devour. You're a temptation I never intend on denying myself. Are you ready?"

"Aye, and take your time." She didn't want to miss a moment of this.

"I shall, my bride." With a groan, he separated her folds and lapped her with his tongue. Pleasure rippled through her and she almost drowned in the storm of sensations to her most sensitive flesh. He suckled her nub, his fingers driving deep inside her and she lost all control, cried out and bucked hard.

Nay, she needed to hold on, to ensure he too felt pleasure just as she did. Under the water, she swept around and found his cock. She wrapped her fingers firm about his shaft and pumped him in long pulls, right in time with how he stroked into her.

"Kyla." He growled her name, circled his fingers inside her in a scintillating way that caused an explosion of heat to build, so swift and so hard. She couldn't hold on a moment longer.

"Come inside me, Ronan. I need you, desperately." Whimpering, she writhed against him.

"Aye, you're ready for me." He lifted her up and dropped her down over top of him in such a fast and deeply penetrating move she almost hurtled from her body. She certainly barely held on to her sanity.

"Oh, goodness, so good." She panted, aching for even more. "Faster."

He drove into her again and again, his pace incredibly wild and raw and exactly as she desired. Her inner muscles contracted and she soared far from her body and flew to the heavens, blissful spasm after spasm rocking through her. Never had she felt so wholly as one with her chosen one. He was hers, always hers.

* * * *

Such a wildly desperate need for his woman rushed through Ronan and as Kyla's hot channel pulsed around him, he thrust balls-deep inside her and roared, his release exploding powerfully along with hers. She was the only woman he'd ever desire, ever crave, and no one would steal her away from him again. He'd make certain of it.

"My mate, my wife, my lover." Against her lips, he whispered the words flowing from his heart, theirs such a heavenly union, one that had joined them together body and soul. "You hold all that I am within you, have become the very air I breathe and the sustenance my body needs."

"As you hold all that I am within you." Tears misted her gaze. "The day I was abducted from the village was the day I gave up the hope I'd ever have a future such as this. Being with you is a dream I never imagined could be possible. Promise me forever."

"I promise you always and forever." From this day forth, wherever they traveled, they'd only do so together. A promise given, and one that would blaze forever within his heart. "Soul bound mates walk the same path. Wherever one goes, so too does the other."

With his woman cradled in his arms and his breathing slowly settling, he carried her out of the water and laid her down on the lush grass underneath the heavy foliage of an elm tree. He needed to ensure he left not one inch of her untouched by his mouth or body, that she experienced all the pleasure he could give her. Rocking over top of her, his cock lengthening all over again, he looked deep into her eyes. "I love you."

"Make me yours again." She dug her fingers into his back, scraped her nails gently down his flesh and he arched into her possessive touch.

Aye, he would. He wanted his chosen one, and with a hunger that held a firm hold on him and would never be appeased. Licking and nibbling, he devoured her breasts, swirled downward and kissed around her belly button, trailed over her hips and along her inner thighs. This was exactly what he needed and when her soft cries for more rang in his ears, he grinned and got drunk at the very heart of her.

"Too much." She gasped and clutched his shoulders, but he

gave her no reprieve.

At her sweet folds, he lapped and rolled around in heaven then once certain she truly couldn't take any more, he lifted up and thrust his cock deep within her.

Sheer bliss took them both, her beautiful breasts rubbing against his chest and her channel gripping him like a fist and dragging him in.

He shuddered as he came, his essence spilling from him and pumping into her, her utter satisfaction at their joining saturating his senses along their merged link, a connection they both clung to.

How had he been so fortunate to have found her after all these years? 'Twas a dream to finally be with her, to know none could ever take her from him again, that he had a lifetime of loving her ahead of him. Slowly, he eased his rocking and she stretched underneath him, her creamy skin glowing under the sunshine streaming through the canopy high above.

With her face in his hands, he captured her mouth and kissed her, sharing his love and all the emotions she'd brought to such fierce life within him. Never had he expected to be gifted with such a woman, their bond forged at the very deepest level.

Aye, they would have an eternity together, his chosen one a woman he'd never release, although as the horn blared moments later from the direction of the beach, the call for their leaving having arrived, he had no choice but to pull himself from her body. He muttered fiercely as he did, but still, this day marked the beginning of the rest of their lives, would be the first of many and the moment he had her back at Carron Castle, he intended on loving her over and over.

He rose to his feet, lifted her to hers and as she searched through the bag of clothing Duncan had given her, he donned a clean shirt from his sack, tucked the hem into a pair of tan rawhide pants and strapped his sword at his side and daggers at each wrist.

"I hope these fit." She pulled out a white tunic and a pair of lad's breeches, held them up against her. "Duncan's squire has gained height and filled out of late."

She donned the billowy tunic, which would do fine, but the beige pants she tugged on were far too big and he removed a belt from his satchel and secured the soft cotton around her hips with the black leather. All he wanted to do was undress her and take her all over again, but instead he packed away their belongings, ran his fingers through her silky golden-red locks and tidied her hair before he ushered her back along the forest trail to the beach and their awaiting kinsmen.

Onboard the galley, the seas calm and the wind fresh, he tucked his chosen one safely under his shoulder as they cruised back to Carron Castle. Aye, he'd finally found the woman who held the other half of his soul, and now he'd always keep her safe. She was his to cherish, his to love, his to always adore.

Chapter 9

Kyla waited in the shadows of Carron's curtain wall for the guard above the postern gate to turn around and return the way he'd come. A month ago, she and Ronan had spoken their vows before Brother Henry who'd traveled to them from the priory. Her mate hadn't wished for her to leave the sanctuary of Coll's keep and had kept her contained right here ever since. Barely had he allowed her more than a stone's throw from his sight or that of a guard's, and although she understood why, she now desperately longed for a moment of freedom. Surely 'twould be possible since she'd spent so much time with Muirin of late in growing her ability.

She could successfully control another's thoughts, had practiced on Cedric several times and he could no longer break her hold. She'd had him dancing up a storm in the courtyard last eve, and for nigh on twenty minutes. The sight of him kicking up his feet had made both her and Fiona fall into a bout of giggles and she'd only released Cedric from her control when Ronan had demanded she take pity on the poor man. In all truth, she could ensure her own protection and all within this keep were well aware of it. Glad she was too that they'd all accepted her fae blood, had welcomed Ronan amongst them. Never had she been so content, or currently impatient.

She tapped one foot as she continued to wait then released a long sigh as the guard finally marched in the other direction and disappeared from her sight. Through the gate, she hurried and dashed along the grassy trail toward the woods. The sun hovered on the horizon, the cool evening breeze washing over her, while across the meadow near the water's edge, dust swirled into the air from the training warriors, their swords clanging and men grunting. They'd soon end their late training session, dive into the loch then return to their barracks to change for the evening meal. She had a half hour, mayhap even an hour to enjoy a swim at the pool and then sneak back into the keep before anyone noticed her missing.

"Kyla!" Ronan shot out from amongst the battling men and chased her, his tan leather pants riding low on his hips and his white shirttails fluttering free. "Halt, now."

"Nay, I want a swim and I've no wish to wait." She snatched the fluttering ribbons of her golden gown as she ducked into the forest. Racing, she bounded over snaking tree roots and sent fallen leaves whisking about, the pool she adored so very close. "I can look after myself and you know it, Ronan Matheson."

"Got you." He swung her up into his arms. "I'm aware you can now look after yourself, but you're still mine to protect."

"Put me down." She slapped his chest. "And you are far too fast for your own good. How on earth did you spy me leaving the keep? You were supposed to be running an errand out by the stables, not training with the men."

"My battle skill has never been stronger since Muirin has aided me in extending my senses. Her knowledge is vast, more so than I could have ever conceived. I might also have misled you a little about my errand. It wasnae at the stables." Grinning, he strode along the trail then emerged from the trees before the pool she completely adored.

"Tell me about your errand." She slapped his chest again for good measure. "Lying is unacceptable."

"My errand brought me right here to this pool." He kissed the tip of her nose. "I caught sight of you trying to escape right after preparing my surprise for you."

"What surprise?" Her heartbeat fluttered within her chest. She adored his surprises and they'd been plenty this past month, all within their chamber and each ensuring they both found such intense pleasure.

"Look ahead." He tipped his head in the direction he meant.

Across the far side of the pool, a fire burned within a small pit of stones and the smoky aroma of cooking meat wafted toward her. "We're to eat out here?"

"I caught a goose, skinned and cleaned it, then set it to cook over the fire. I thought you might enjoy some time outside under the stars with me. We can eat then swim." Overhead, the sun began its descent and sent a blaze of red into the darkening blue, the fiery color turning his golden eyes a smoldering hue.

"I love being outside with you."

"Good." He set her down on his tartan spread before the fire, eased in behind her and rested his chin on the top of her head. "If you wish for more freedom, I can grant it. Your skill is far stronger than ever afore and I'm a little less on edge now because of it."

"More freedom would be perfect." Skirts tucked under her legs, she leaned back against him and embraced his warmth as the skies darkened even further and the moon rose within the heavenly blanket of black above.

"No more sneaking out though. You'll tell me where you wish to go, or if I'm no' about then a guard, although you cannae wander any farther than this pool. Do we have an agreement?"

"We do." She rubbed her back against his chest and surrounded herself in his heat. "Have you received any word from my parents yet?" The day they'd returned from Rhue, he'd sent a messenger with a missive detailing all that had occurred and she'd written a letter as well which had gone with his note. If only she could cross the distance separating her from her parents and connect to their minds with her skill. She itched to be able to do so, hoped it would be possible soon. Muirin had said 'twas only a matter of time should she continue with her training, of which she'd been determined to master.

"No additional word, other than their original reply. They know you live, that you've spoken vows with me and that I'll remain right here at your side guarding you. The moment they can travel safely to Carron's shores for a visit, they shall."

"Now that I know I might be able to see them soon, I can barely stand the wait."

"So I've noticed. Here, the meat looks cooked." He leaned past her, set the skewered meat to one side of the fire to cool, slid her hair over her shoulder and nuzzled her neck. "While it cools, I'll distract you."

"Oh, I do love a good distraction." More than loved it and as he eased back and took her with him to lie flat on the ground, his form of distraction turned into a slow and sensual seduction that soon sent her flying from her body and soaring amongst the brilliance of the stars as they came out to play.

'Twas the most enchanting night, his surprise the best she'd ever had.

* * * *

A week later and on the tips of her toes, Kyla tried to shove past Ronan's broad back as they waited at Carron's sea-gate landing after she'd successfully reconnected with Mama after Muirin had aided her in extending her skill's range. Their long-awaited conversation had lasted right through the night, both of them talking over the other with all the news they'd wished to share, a lifetime of such, then after speaking to Mama, she'd connected with Papa and tears of giddy excitement and joy had streamed down her cheeks.

Now, with a sudden break in the warring across their lands and the isles, her parents had been able to board a galley Duncan had captained to their village. They were here, really here.

Papa, in a forest-green tunic and leather pants, aided Mama out of the vessel, her golden-red hair now holding the odd strand of gray but her face as youthful as ever.

With a squeal, Mama cried out, her teal gown with its long lace tapered sleeves flapping as she rushed along the landing toward her.

"Mama, Papa!" She ran right into Mama's open arms and another flood of tears streaked down her cheeks, Mama's too as they mashed their wet cheeks together. "I'm so glad you're both here."

"We've been waiting for what feels like forever to see you, my sweet. You look so well."

"And tall." Papa chuckled and wrapped his arms around them both. "You've grown somewhat. A wee lass you are no more."

"Tell me how your new husband is treating you." Mama dotted her forehead with kisses, each one making her heart swell fuller with love.

"Extremely well." She smiled mischievously over her shoulder at Ronan, who stood with his chest pumped out and his grin wide. "Come here, my mate."

"Welcome to Carron Castle, Grace, Isaiah." He joined them, gripped Papa's hand and hugged Mama. "Thank you both for giving me your daughter. I consider myself the most fortunate man alive."

"'Tis truly a miracle our Christina—I mean Kyla has now been found and most grateful I am you've brought her safely back to us." Mama squeezed Ronan tight then cupped her face, peered into her eyes. "Since I never saw your death, I always held the hope that you lived. I certainly wish I'd heard that the Chief of MacKenzie had taken in a lost child and claimed her as his foster daughter. That news never reached us."

"He kept it very quiet, only those within his keep ever aware. Have you explained all to Papa?"

"I have now, and we'll both keep Coll and Duncan's secret safe. One day they will be ready to share the truth with one and all, but until that day arrives, neither of us shall whisper a word."

"Then come. 'Tis time for you to see Carron Castle." She looped her arm through Mama's and led her along the landing and up the stone stairs, her heart overflowing with happiness, Papa and Ronan one step behind them.

Aye, this day marked a new beginning, one in which she now had her parents back.

No more lost kin. Never again.

'Twas time for the fae to live.

Chapter 10

Sprawled naked across Ronan's chest within their golden canopied bed at Carron Castle, the warmth from the crackling fireplace washing over her, Kyla had never felt so blissfully at rest, no matter the late hour of the night.

"I'm surprised Isaiah and Grace finally allowed us to leave the great hall." Ronan played his fingers through her hair, his muscled body rippling with strength underneath hers.

"You tossed me over your shoulder and carted me upstairs so fast you didnae even give them a chance to wrestle you to the ground as they did last eve." A week her parents had been here and during that time they'd all become so much closer.

"I'm getting faster, wiser, and more devious." He caught her hand and threaded their fingers together before running one thumb over her sparkling sapphire and diamond ring, the gold band having been adjusted by the armorer and its fit now perfect.

"Speaking of being devious." She wriggled up, hooked one leg over his hips and straddled him. Such intense emotions swamped her, the most wondrous of all being love. It filled her heart and overflowed it. "I'm expecting."

"Pardon?"

"We're going to have a family of our own."

"Are you certain?" He stared at her flat belly then with slightly shaky hands, rested his palms gently upon her, his touch so reverent. "I see naught."

"I'm very certain since I've no' had my courses since you returned to claim me. We will be parents ourselves afore too long."

"Incredible." A smile lifted his lips as he traced around her breasts then lifted up, his elbows pressed into the mattress as he swept his tongue over one nipple and then the other. "Your breasts are fuller. That I most definitely noticed."

"They are?"

"Deliciously so." He sucked her nipple deep inside his mouth and flicked the tip with his tongue before toppling her onto her back and thrusting inside of her so fast, she almost came from his fiercely powerful stroke alone. She certainly fought to hold onto her control, her body tingling the entire length where they touched.

Gasping for breath, she arched her back, tried to speak only he moved so deeply inside her that she hadn't a chance of forming a word. With no other choice, she gave herself fully over to their love, held onto him in every way, with both her body and her mind.

Aye, since the day of her birth, she'd been bound to him and would be until the very end of time. Her mate, her chosen one, the man who'd made her his bride.

Chapter 11

Standing cloaked and unseen on the battlements of Carron Castle, Cherub gazed out over the rippling waters of Loch Carron with Kirk at her back, his deliciously strong arms wrapped snugly around her. The full moon blazed within the midnight sky and the air swirled and brought to her all the secrets it held.

Soon a new day would dawn, one overflowing with an abundance of hope as never before. Ronan and Kyla, currently ensconced in their chamber while the rest of their kin feasted in the great hall, had begun to bridge the gap between two warring clans, and now 'twas most certainly time for the fae to live. Duncan and Coll included.

"Ronan has completed his hunt. Where to next, my elusive imp?" Kirk twirled her around to face him then smothered her in his heavenly heat, his body a shield of strength around hers. "Do you sense any more lost souls this night?"

"I do, and that of two men, one right here at Carron Castle and the other still searching MacKenzie land in his quest to gather more warriors to his cause."

"You mean Duncan and Coll?"

"Aye, they've been so loyal to their fae kind even though I

never knew it, and they shall be the ones to lead clan MacKenzie forward into a new future, although soon they'll feel the urge to seek out their chosen ones and when they do, you and I will be right here on hand to guide them in the right direction. 'Tis time they learnt more about their mother's Matheson clan, that we fae always stand beside our own. Beth may no' be here to care for them, but we are."

"Then this is one mission I cannae wait for." He seized her mouth with his, his desire flaring hot and strong, the same as her desire flared for him.

"Neither can I." She laughed and sent them both soaring high into the skies and toward the radiant stars above, her heart and soul singing at the incredible joy of having her chosen one with her. This is what she wanted for all of her fae kind, for them to bind their mates to them, her duty one she'd never release.

Aye, aiding both Duncan and Coll in their coming hunts would be a chase of the most delicious sort. What a journey those two men had ahead of them, one of discovery and love, of learning when to battle, and when to accept fate.

Sweet love. May it soon be theirs too.

Author's Note

In the twelfth century, clan Matheson settled around the area of Loch Alsh, Loch Carron, and Kintail, and gave their allegiance to clan MacDonald whose chiefs were the Lords of the Isles. Clan Matheson became a large and powerful clan with a force of around two-thousand men, although by the middle of the sixteenth century they'd diminished greatly in size and influence due to the blood feuds raging across the isles at that time. This warring left them to possess less than a third of their original Matheson property on Loch Alsh.

It's also well known in history that clan Matheson also forged an alliance with clan MacKenzie during the middle ages, which meant at times the two clans fought side by side, yet also against each other when clan Matheson found themselves stuck in the middle of the feuding between the MacDonalds and the MacKenzies. Within this series my hope is to capture the difficulties faced between these two great clans, and all while spinning stories in my own unique way.

Certainly across all the books I've written involving the three clans of Matheson, MacKenzie, and MacDonald, I've tried my best to show how their feuding and alliances made, moved back and forth throughout the years. I dearly love all these clans, can understand their struggles and losses, their conquests and wins, as well as how they attempted to remain as honorable as they could throughout it all.

This story is woven with as much accuracy to the period and locations as possible, although any mistakes made are mine alone. Please feel free to search for any of my other works. I simply adore strong heroines, and have a ton of fun matching them with their honorable alpha heroes.

**Also available in paperback
Scottish Historical Romance**

Traveling through time…for a Highlander.

Highlander Heat Series

Highlander's Castle, Book One

Highlander's Magic, Book Two

Highlander's Charm, Book Three

Highlander's Guardian, Book Four

Highlander's Faerie, Book Five

Highlander's Champion, Book Six

by Joanne Wadsworth

Looking for more sexy Scottish adventure?

Catch a teaser excerpt of the next book in this series.

Highlander's Caress

The Matheson Brothers, Book Eight

by Joanne Wadsworth

Highlander's Caress

The Matheson Brothers, Book Eight

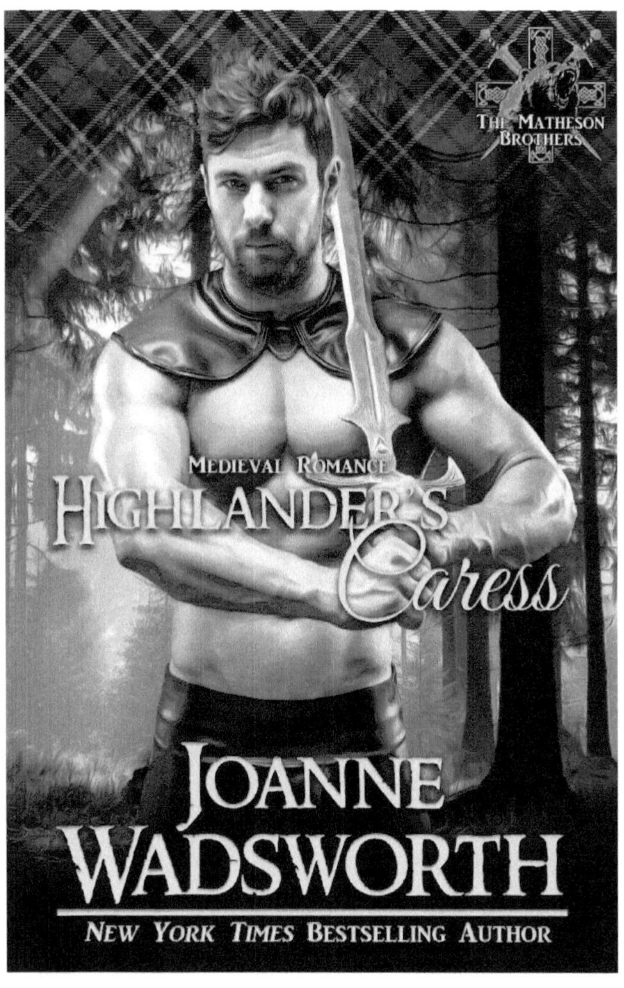

Teaser Excerpt

"Playing with you could be dangerous, Duncan." Although unable to help herself, Ella shuffled forward in her seat. Making the first move, she selected a chess piece and slid it across the board and into position. Aye, naught more did she thrive on than coming up against a new opponent, and Duncan MacKenzie made one very fine one at that.

"Yet you're a fae compeller, while I'm merely a warrior with the ability to wield a blade. It should be me who says playing with you could be dangerous." He moved his chosen piece, the fire's glow flickering across his high cheeks.

"Aye, with one word I could alter this game."

"You would cheat against me?" Moving swiftly, he reached across, nabbed her woolen cap from her head and dropped it into her lap before easing back and eyeing her long locks as they swished down and swayed about her waist. "My apologies, but I needed to see more of you."

"I'll certainly cheat if you do that again." He had the reflexes of a warrior, swift and precise and she'd best not forget it. She wound her hair back up and stuffed her cap overtop of it, tugged the wool down good and proper so he couldn't so easily do that again. "So, would you truly have wed the MacDonald's daughter to end this current feud?"

"Aye, do you no' agree a marriage of alliance would have been worthwhile?"

"Such marriages arenae the way of my clan. We wait for our chosen one to claim us then join only with them."

"I'm aware of how your people join together when mated." He searched her gaze. "Are you wed, Ella, or do you still await your chosen one?"

"I wait, as patiently as I can."

"What if he never comes?"

"He will."

"You have such faith." Gently, he laid his hand over top of hers and whispered, "Turn your hand over."

For some reason she did, until their palms lay flush together and a new warmth enveloped her and rippled outward from her core.

With the softest caress, he stroked her palm with his thumb in one very slow, enticing circle, his gaze holding hers and not wavering one bit. "You, Ella, are the most intriguing lass I've ever met."

The Matheson Brothers Continued

Highlander's Kiss, Book Four
Highlander's Heart, Book Five
Highlander's Sword, Book Six

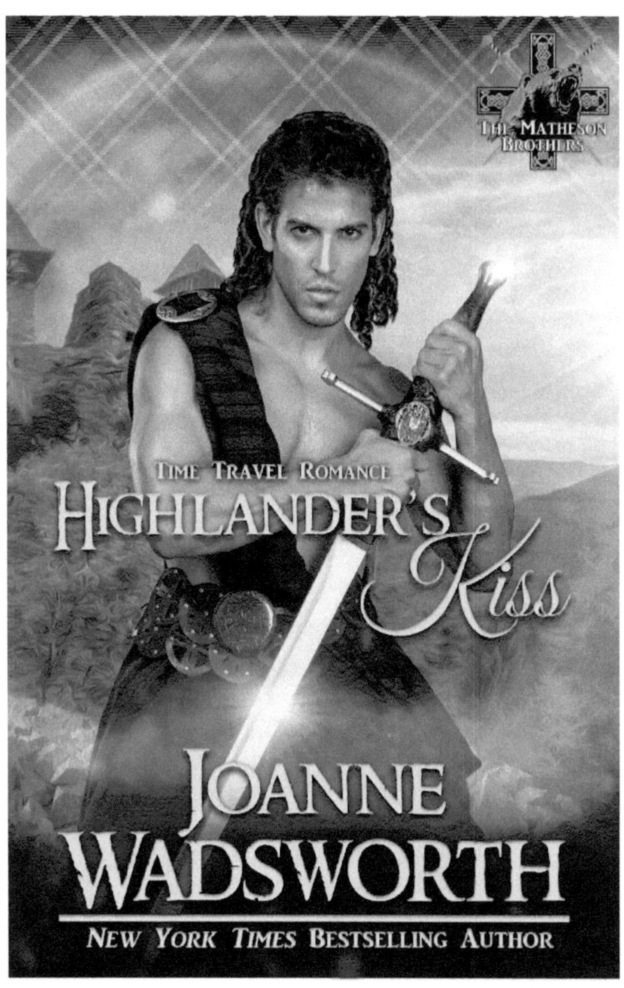

The Matheson Brothers Continued

Highlander's Shifter, Book Ten
Highlander's Claim, Book Eleven
Highlander's Courage, Book Twelve
Highlander's Mermaid, Book Thirteen

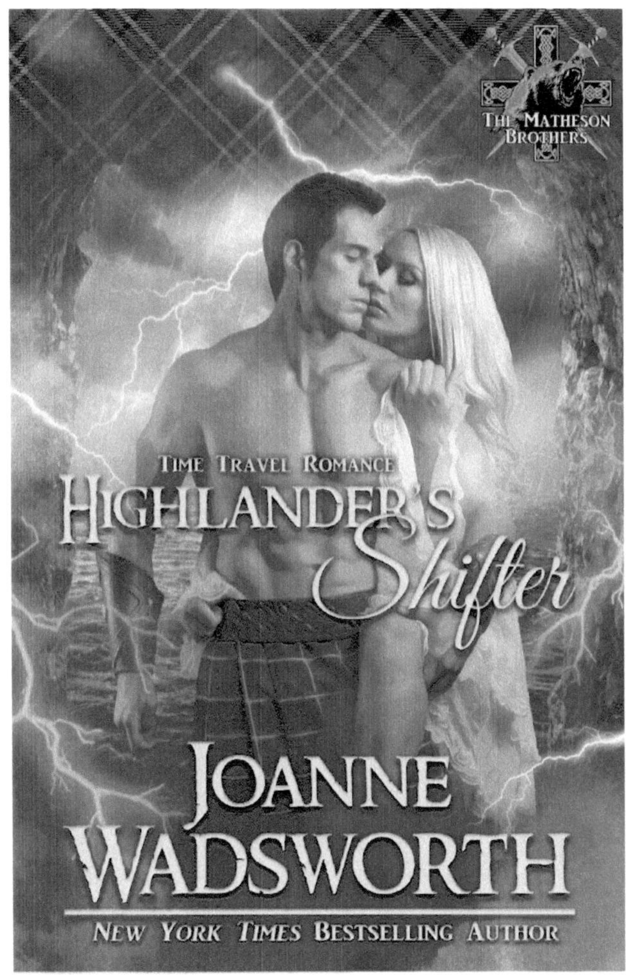

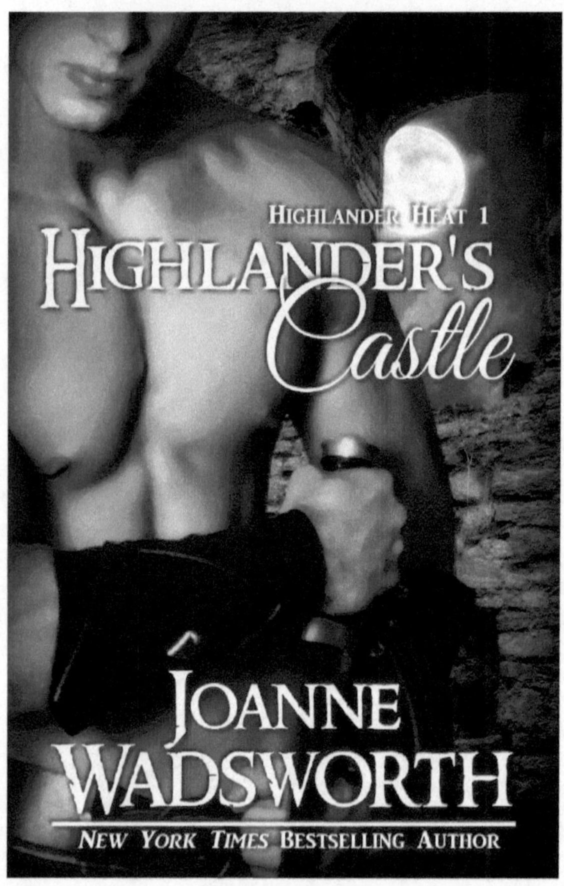

HIGHLANDER HEAT 1
HIGHLANDER'S
Castle
JOANNE
WADSWORTH
NEW YORK TIMES BESTSELLING AUTHOR

Regency Brides

The Duke's Bride, Book One
The Earl's Bride, Book Two
The Wartime Bride, Book Three
The Earl's Secret Bride, Book Four
The Prince's Bride, Book Five
Her Pirate Prince, Book Six

Billionaire Bodyguards

Billionaire Bodyguard Attraction, Book One
Billionaire Bodyguard Boss, Book Two
Billionaire Bodyguard Fling, Book Three

JOANNE WADSWORTH

Joanne Wadsworth is a *New York Times* and *USA Today* Bestselling Author who adores getting lost in the world of romance, no matter what era in time that might be. Hot alpha Highlanders hound her, demanding their stories are told and she's devoted to ensuring they meet their match, whether that be with a feisty lass from the present or far in the past.

Living on a tiny island at the bottom of the world, she calls New Zealand home. Big-dreamer, hoarder of chocolate, and addicted to juicy watermelons since the age of five, she chases after her four energetic children and has her own hunky hubby on the side.

So come and join in all the fun, because this kiwi girl promises to give you her "Hot-Highlander" oath, to bring you a heart-pounding, sexy adventure from the moment you turn the first page. This is where romance meets fantasy and adventure…

To learn more about Joanne and her works, visit
http://www.joannewadsworth.com

www.ingramcontent.com/pod-product-compliance
Lightning Source LLC
Chambersburg PA
CBHW051228210726
48290CB00003B/857